Mutual Obsession

CHARISSE C. CARR

Prologue

HAROLD "GRAMPS" DEEDS

"This isn't somethin' we wanted for you, grandson. I understand you wanna follow in our footsteps, but when your father and I controlled these streets, it was durin' a different time. This generation is shot to hell and very disrespectful. The people we worked for require a certain level of respect and complete honesty. They won't hesitate to end your life and those of the ones you love."

I was sitting in the kitchen explaining to my grandson Grayson, who everyone called Gray, about the pros and cons of being a bill collector for the streets. During my reign, I didn't need a team or someone else with me that I had to be accountable for. Harold Deeds was a one man wrecking machine, like Denzel Washington in the *Equalizer*. When I collected my payment, it all belonged to me.

1

My only son, Hudson, replaced me once I decided to enjoy the fruits of my labor. He learned from the best. Therefore, you couldn't even tell there was a changing of the guards. Hudson picked up right where I left off. Unfortunately, his life came to a sudden end, unrelated to his line of work.

When my wife and I were tasked with raising his son, we wanted more for our grandson. It was our vision for Gray to go to college and live a normal life, away from the streets. But like the Deeds, this lifestyle came natural to him.

"Gramps, I get that, but this is what I want. When the right woman comes into my life, years from now, I promise to hang it up and give you and Big Mama a gang of great-grands. Until then, teach me everythin' I need to know to continue the legacy of the Deeds. The streets are talkin', and the niggas that took ova after dad ain't it. They been disappearin' left and right ova the years 'cause they got their hand in the cookie jar, lyin' 'bout people not payin' and shit. And the ones that are on the up and up, are bein' killed by the very people they supposed to be collectin' from 'cause they unorganized," Gray argued.

"And that's my point. If somethin' happens to you, then I gotta make the streets bleed and move yo grandma away from here after I burn this muthafucka down. And that's if she don't take me out first for not protectin' you," I explained.

"That ain't gone happen. Bear and Ant got my back, and all three of us together would be unstoppable." Gray stared me dead in my eyes, looking just like his father. "And these niggas respect you enough to know not to come for me. Our name still rings heavy in these streets and carries much weight."

"Listen, you only sixteen years old. If we do this, you have to be in the best shape physically and mentally. You can't just run up on niggas, demandin' the money owed to yo clients. It takes patience and skill to know when and how to strike. Always make sure you stalk yo target and know the ins and outs of their operation. Never, under no circumstances, let 'em know you comin'. Just show up, unannounced, at the opportune time and take what's yours."

Gray sat back in his chair and grinned.

"So, does this mean you gone train me?"

"Yes, and when I feel you are ready, I'll introduce you to the clients I know and trust. Yo grandma will keep yo books 'til you find someone you trust wit' yo life to do it. Once you're eighteen, you'll invest in a business. I have only one rule, and if you break it, I'll snatch the rug right from underneath yo feet. Don't ever think you know more than me. That's the rule. What I say goes. I told yo father the same."

"Gramps, my word is my bond. I will honor you 'til the day our time together comes to an end, which is no time soon. You're the teacher, and I'm the student. I'll neva get those two confused."

I got a little choked up when Gray spoke those words.

"Yo father said the same exact thin' to me. Whew... I know he lives on in you. Go the fuck on before you make a grown man cry. Love you, grandson."

"Love you too, Gramps. And thanks. I'mma make you proud."

"Too late, you did that the day you were born."

3

I took a deep breath and shook my head. It was time for me to come out of retirement for a little bit.

Chapter One

GRAYSON "GRAY" DEEDS

TEN YEARS LATER...

"Listen, I told you niggas I wasn't nothin' to play wit'. You muthafuckas must have been hearin' impaired that day, so let me check y'all other senses and see if they any betta. Let's start with eyesight."

I walked over to Tommy, who was currently laying face first on the dance floor of his club in between his two business partners. They owed my client 300k. My team and I were here to collect. Bear and Ant had their guns pointed, locked and loaded, ready to send anyone of these cornball ass niggas on a permanent trip to the afterlife.

Crouching down by his head, I let out a long sigh.

"Put your right hand in front of you, spread it out, and tell me how many fingers you see." I waited for Tommy to respond.

"Five," he mumbled.

I raised the eleven inch machete I was holding in the air and brought it down, cutting off his pinky and ring fingers.

"Tell me how many you see now?"

"Ahhhhhhh, you fuckin' bitch ass nigga!" Tommy yelled, grabbing the wrist of his bloody hand.

"I've been called worse," I responded, shrugging my shoulders. "Answer the question. Otherwise, I'll take the whole damn hand off."

"Three." Tommy spoke through clenched teeth.

"Now, where is the money you were supposed to have waiting for me? I warned you the last time I came in this hole in the wall you call a club not to make me have to ask for it twice."

I wiped the machete clean on top of Tommy's bald head before standing back up.

"Like I just told you, man. I don't—" I kicked him in the face, cutting him off.

Tommy spit the blood that spilled into his mouth from his nose onto the floor.

"Yeah, that salty, metallic taste is disgustin'. So far we know you have selective hearin', you can see and count, and you don't like the taste of yo own blood. Now, we need to see if you can smell the smoke before you feel the fire when I burn this bitch down wit' y'all in it," I threatened.

"Okay, okay, don't burn it down, please. I only have half the money in the safe in the back office," Tommy admitted.

"What's the code?"

Once he said the code out loud, Bear went to retrieve the cash.

"I can have the rest for you in a couple weeks. Just let me go, so I can get to the hospital."

"A couple weeks? Nigga, you ain't on no easy payment plan. We not Klarna or Sezzle." I laughed.

"Can you at least put my fingers on ice?"

"Hell no! Fuck you and them fingers," I answered.

"It was exactly half the amount he owed in there, nothing else," Bear informed me when he came back to the dance floor area.

"What's the odds of that? I think he playin' in our face and never planned on givin' us the full amount." I kissed my teeth.

"I told yo punk ass this wasn't gone work," Tommy's business partner to the left of him spewed.

"Shut the fuck up, nigga."

"Nah, I need all my fingers. Gray, I know where the rest of the money is. I had nothing to do wit' this shit. Believe me, I know how you get down and wanted no part in tryin' to deceive you."

This muthafucka was selling his soul to the devil without even being asked.

"Well, if you know where the money is at and willin' to hand it over, I guess there's no need to keep yo friends around, right?"

"Right," he responded without any hesitation.

"I gave Ant a nod, and he put a bullet in the back of their heads."

"Oh, shit... fuck, man."

"Aht, aht, aht, don't do that. This is what you wanted." I smirked.

"Umm, yeah, it's just—"

"Just what?" I cut him off. "This is business, nigga. We not playin' no fuckin' games. Our time is valuable. Now, talk, so we can get up outta here."

He told us the money was hidden inside an empty fridge Tommy kept in the office with an out of order sign on it. It was right in plain sight. After Bear and Ant packed all the money up in duffle bags, I told the one remaining member of the trio to stand up.

"Since you owned a third of the club, this was just as much yo debt as it was theirs. My client had the pills y'all sold in here delivered, but you muthafuckas refused to pay him, claimin' y'all neva received the shipment. We all know that was a lie, right?"

The pills were sent via FedEx, disguised as vitamins. The tracking showed it was signed for upon delivery, and the guy who dropped off the package secretly took a pic of the box sitting on the bar in the club, with Tommy in the background, to cover his ass. This wasn't the first time muthafuckas tried to lie on him.

"Tommy said he was tired of yo client increasin' the price without notice, expectin' us to just pay."

"You weak. I don't like weak people. With a nigga like you

in their circle, there was no room for an enemy. Instead of sinkin' wit' the ship as it was goin' down, you decided to bail out. And yo ass is still tryna swim toward the shore by runnin' yo mouth. In this line of work, loyalty is everythin', and you have none."

Before he could get another word out and try to plead his case, I decapitated his ass. We watched as his head dropped and rolled like an apple falling from a tree.

"I'mma call the cleanup crew," Ant informed me.

"Tell 'em the money will be in the fridge. How much was in there?" I questioned.

"600k, can you believe that shit," Bear responded, shaking his head.

"Yeah, I can. He stood on business and refused to pay, even though he had it. It cost Tommy his life, but I respect him. Unlike this headless ass nigga."

"That muthafucka really thought he was walkin' out of here." Ant laughed.

"Not realizin' their fate was sealed the minute we walked in and didn't see the money." I turned my attention to Bear. "Leave 40k for the crew. This surveillance system isn't that hi-tech."

We always paid the cleanup crew we used 10k per body, plus the cost of destroying all the footage. If I needed them to burn the bitch down, it was an extra 10k. Today was lightwork for them.

As one of the most ruthless bill collectors for the organizations that operated above the law, I made a pretty good living for myself. Bear and Ant were twin brothers who had been my best friends from our playground days. They definitely had different personalities, which was why I gave them nicknames that everyone eventually started using.

I couldn't tell them apart for years, so I based it on how they acted. Bear was laid back and was down for whatever when it came to us, otherwise he stayed to himself. He was very protective, especially over me, since I was the smallest out of us growing up. Now, I stood at six foot two with an athletic build, but these niggas were six foot four and around 250 pounds of pure muscle. So, imagine them as kids. They looked like two human, Everlast punching bags. Even though his physical presence was imposing, like a bear, he was a gentle giant unless you poked him.

Ant was annoying like a damn ant and couldn't sit his ass still. He never made a move without us, though. Whatever he did was always for the benefit of our circle. The most social out of the three of us, Ant was always the life of the party. All the ladies loved his outgoing personality, which was great for Bear and I because we never had to go looking for a good time. It always came to us through Ant.

"It's still early. What's on the agenda for the rest of the day?" Ant quizzed.

I looked down at my watch and realized it was five o'clock.

"Shit, early for you. If I'm not on time for Sunday dinner, Big Mama gone cuss my ass out. She used to have the food done by three. I had to beg her to change it to six," I admitted.

"You know old people don't play 'bout Sunday dinner. They like to be in bed by six," Bear joked.

"Say less... I'm followin' yo ass when we leave, so I can get some real food. Big Mama won't mind." Ant smiled.

"Nigga, ain't yo baby momma cookin' and invitin' her parents over to y'all house?" Bear reminded him.

"Fuck you, since you tryna be funny. You know her ass can't cook. I'm not eatin' that shit. When I get there, I will be full as hell and goin' straight to bed. Kira know we not together like that but keep puttin' on a front for her peoples to save face."

Ant was the only one who had settled down and had a kid. Him and his girl stayed at it, though. He said they were just roommates at this point, but she still wanted the relationship. Their daughter was only two years old, so he said she could still live there, but they slept in separate rooms.

"Well, let's go. It's startin' to stink in here," I complained.

"You lucky yo ass walked in when you did 'cause I was about to be upset. I like to serve my food hot, and you know that." Big Mama cut her eyes at me.

"I'm yo only grandson, don't do me like that." I kissed Big Mama on the cheek as she stirred the homemade gravy. You could smell it as soon as you crossed the threshold of the front door.

"Oh, yeah, fried chicken wit' all the sides. And I see a peach cobbler cooling in the window." Ant started dancing.

Bear said he would get up with us later. He wanted to make sure the cleanup crew showed up on time and chose to wait for them in his truck in the parking lot. The club was closed on Sundays, which was why we chose today to meet back up there. No one else should be showing up, but Bear was overly cautious, and I loved that about him.

"Who invited yo greedy ass?"

"Don't do me like that, Big Mama." Ant faked like he was sad.

"Come give me some suga, boy." Big Mama smiled and hugged him. "It's always good to see you. One of y'all is missin'."

"Bear had to handle some business, so he'll come by next time," I explained.

"I thought I heard some riff-raffs down here."

"Don't start yo shit, Harold." Big Mama yelled at her husband as he entered the kitchen.

"Shut yo big ass up, Henrietta. I can joke wit' my grandson, and his freeloadin' ass friend."

"Wassup, Gramps. What were you upstairs doin'?" I quizzed.

Usually he was already down here, getting on Big Mama nerves.

"Playin' wit' my balls, lil nigga."

Ant and I laughed, but Big Mama blew her breath. She hated the way he talked, but loved everything else about him. They argued all day long, then would spend the rest of the night fooling around like teenagers. A love like theirs was rare, and

I'm glad I got to witness it. Hopefully, one day I would find a woman like Big Mama, who'd make me as happy as she made Gramps.

My dad, Hudson Deeds, was murdered when I was five by his best friend. He was their only child. They said it was over my mom, Carla, but she would rather die before admitting that shit. Hudson confronted his friend after the streets kept talking about him being involved with my mom. He had his suspicions already and saw some text messages between the two that looked inappropriate as hell. They ended up getting physical outside on the basketball courts in front of everyone. After my dad beat the shit out of him, his friend shot him in the back as he walked away.

Big Mama said my mom was always crazy, but the death of my dad pushed her over the edge. She dropped me off to them one weekend and never came back to get me. Throughout the years, my mom stopped by on holidays and my birthday, whenever she wasn't locked up or in a mental institution. The interactions between her and my grandparents always felt awkward, but I didn't understand until I got older and learned about what transpired. They blamed my mom for their son's death.

I knew it had to be hard for them to let the woman, who still wouldn't own her truth, into their home. As a teenager, I heard Gramps tell Big Mama the only reason she was still breathing was because of their love for me, and I didn't deserve to be an orphaned child due to no fault of my own. He meant that shit too. Back in the day, Gramps ran these streets, which was why they never questioned the lifestyle I chose. It was in my DNA. I learned everything from him, the original bill collector.

Everyone respected Gramps, which is why they refused to move from this house and neighborhood. I tried to buy them a new home in a gated community, but Big Mama and Gramps told me to save my money for my own family. Money wasn't an issue for me, though. For the last eight years I've been stacking. My clients gave me thirty percent of whatever I collected, which I split evenly amongst my guys. I couldn't do what I do without them.

If any extra money was discovered, like today, we pocketed that for ourselves. So, not only did we secure the 300k owed to my client, but Bear, Ant, and I got to split an extra $260k after we paid the cleanup crew. Just to make sure we covered our asses, each of us opened businesses that were very lucrative. I owned four laundromats and two drive-thru car washes in central Jersey. The first thing Gramps taught me was to make my life appear normal.

I knew he had money stashed away and didn't need the help I always offered. From the outside looking in, you would never know it. They weren't flashy and didn't draw attention to themselves. Gramps owned a few auto body shops. Big Mama was a housewife, who liked to garden and cook. No one knew she was the backbone of the operation, accepting and denying jobs while keeping the books. They gave the lifestyle up once my dad took over the family business.

Gramps and Big Mama never lied or tried to hide who they were from me because they knew I would find out eventually.

Gramps also wanted me to be informed and aware of my surroundings, just in case any of the people whose lives he affected during his reign tried to seek revenge on him through me.

The organizations Gramps connected me with were more than happy to have another Deeds back in the mix. Everyone they had collecting for them wasn't honest or efficient as we were.

"You got a trash ass mouth." Big Mama tucked in her bottom lip.

"Ah, hell, yo ass just mad you ain't playin' wit' 'em," Gramps shot back.

"Keep talkin' shit, and I'mma cut those shriveled up, lopsided muthafuckas off. They went from plump plums to raggedy raisins."

Big Mama grabbed the knife she had laying on the counter and playfully shook it.

"And yo pussy went from a fierce mountain lion to a malnourished alley cat. It don't even purr anymore, just sputters like an old car. The motor is dead."

"Y'all wildin'. We 'bout to head outside real quick," I informed them after giving Ant a head nod.

"Dinner will be ready in ten minutes," Big Mama yelled as we exited the kitchen.

As soon as we got outside on the porch, I pulled the pre-rolled blunt from behind my ear and lit it, taking a couple pulls before passing it to Ant.

"I wished my grandparents' house was as funny as yours,

bruh. There's neva a dull moment 'round here wit' those two."
Ant laughed, passing the blunt back.

"Man, Gramps and Big Mama are my hearts in human form. My momma side basically said fuck me, but not them. Usually the daddy side of the family got the bad rap. This time the tables were turned. One of my aunts actually had the nerve to ask me for some money the other day. I haven't communicated wit' her in years, but she sends me a DM out of nowhere. I left that muthafucka on read, so she knows I saw it."

"Who? Sharon's funky ass? I know it was her. Every once in a while I see her down at the racetrack, beggin' and shit. I gave her fifty dollars one day 'cause I knew she was yo auntie," Ant admitted.

"Yup. I see her in passin', but she never sees me. If it wasn't for social media, none of those niggas would even know what I looked like." I shook my head.

"My family fucked up too, both sides, so you not alone." Ant reached for the blunt.

Just as I handed it to him, Rain pulled up into the driveway next door and hopped out of her car after killing the engine. She came over every Sunday to have dinner with her parents, who had been our neighbors for as long as I can remember. This woman made my heart skip a beat every time I laid eyes on her. Even though Rain was spoken for, I always told her she would be mine one day.

"Hey, big head." Rain smiled at me.

"Wassup, beautiful. Where that corny ass nigga of yours?" I quizzed.

"You always got jokes." She gave me the finger. "I don't know who's worse, you or Gramps."

Besides me, Bear, and Ant, Rain was the only other person who called my grandparents by the nicknames I gave them. They watched her grow up. She was my female best friend.

"The fact that his ass ain't neva invited to Sunday dinner should tell you everythin' you need to know. I'm the man you need in yo life. Yo parents love me." I licked my lips and smirked at her.

"Whateva. Hey, Ant." Rain waved at him.

"I wondered when yo ass was gonna acknowledge me. Did you give Harmony my number?" Ant questioned.

"No... don't nobody got time to be fightin' yo crazy ass baby momma. Gray, I'll holla at you before I leave. You stayin' the night, right?"

"Yeah, text me." Rain walked off and went into the house.

I always spent the night on Sundays. It was a tradition I started when I moved out and got my own spot. We turned the basement into a studio apartment, so it was my home away from home. It even had its own entrance on the side of the house. No matter what I did or where I went in this life, Sundays would always be reserved for Big Mama and Gramps.

Chapter Two

RAIN ELLINGTON

"Hey, mom and dad." I called out to my parents as I used my key to enter their house.

"Hey to you too, sweet girl," my mom, Deborah, greeted me.

She was standing in the living room with a dish towel thrown over her right shoulder, peeking out the front window.

"Are you expectin' someone else?" I questioned.

"Nope... I heard your car door shut, but when you didn't come right in, I wondered what, or should I say who, held you up." She grinned.

"Oh, yeah, I was talkin' to Gray and Ant." I smiled.

"I'm surprised you two never hooked up. You know Gray is crazy about you. He's a much better choice than that damn Jamal," my mom expressed.

Jamal and I started dating during our sophomore year of high school, but didn't get serious until the following year. He was my first everything, and even though he didn't always treat me the best, Jamal was my comfort zone. After high school, we moved in together, against my parent's wishes. They planned for me to go away to a HBCU, but I was so in love and didn't want to leave my man.

I went to our local university while Jamal worked a bunch of dead end jobs, until my dad finally offered him a position at his construction company. My parents only agreed to give him a job because they were sick of having to give me extra money to cover his portion of the bills. They made sure to let me know my room was waiting for me whenever I had enough of raising a grown ass man. After graduation, I started my career in nursing.

Even with everything on course financially, Jamal still found a way to make life hard for us by flirting with other women at work, like it wouldn't get back to my dad. Once I confronted him about it, Jamal started coming home later and later, saying he needed to clear his mind after working all day. My parents finally put their foot down when I confided in them about Jamal's suspicious behavior and said he wasn't allowed in their home anymore.

The only reason Jamal kept his job was because I begged my dad not to fire him. I was their only child and the apple of my dad's eye. There was nothing he wouldn't do for me. They knew I wasn't going to leave him and didn't want me to pick up the slack financially.

My sister from another mister, Harmony, hated Jamal and

sided with my parents. They all wanted better for me, but I was afraid of starting over and didn't want to be alone. Along with Gray, every dude in our hood wanted me. I knew I was a catch and had other options, but there was a side to me that very few knew about. Jamal never judged or treated me differently, so I felt like he was my soulmate, even though no one else did.

"Gray is like the brother I neva had. I value our friendship too much to cross that line. He is fine, though. I'll admit that. That scrawny lil kid who always called me names and put worms in my head grew into a sexy man. And I don't like his career choice, so it wouldn't work." I shrugged.

"I don't particularly mind that he's continuing the Deed's family business. Your father and I would never have to worry about you another day in our lives if you were with him. Gray has always been respectful, treated you like royalty, besides the worms and name calling as kids, and he would provide you the type of life you deserve. The kind that your dad provides for me. And the fact that he's easy on the eyes is a plus. Jamal, not so much. Now, give me my hug." We embraced before I headed into the bathroom to wash my hands.

Jamal wasn't the cutest guy, but he wasn't ugly, ugly. I tried to get him to workout with me, but he was satisfied with his bulky build. Even though I was a solid size sixteen myself, I went to the gym three days a week to tone. All my weight was in my hips, ass, and breast. I did have a few rolls in the waist and auntie arms, but my 5' 8" frame held it all together well. Plus, I did a lot of walking at work, getting my cardio in.

When I came out of the bathroom, my dad was helping my

mom bring the food to the dining room. Even though it was only three of us, my parents always made Sunday dinner special and went all out. It was a time for us to love on each other and catch up on what's been happening with the Ellingtons.

"There's my sweet girl." My dad's smile brightened the whole room as he wrapped me in his arms. He always gave the best hugs. "Of all the things I've built in this life, you are my greatest creation."

"Awe, dad, I love you."

"I love you more. How have you been?" he inquired, pulling out my chair.

"Great. I'm thinkin' of takin' a permanent position on the pediatric floor at the hospital. I floated there a few times and loved it." I took a sip of the water that was already poured up in a glass.

"Are you sure? Seeing kids sick all the time isn't an easy task." My mom raised her brows.

"That's the reason why I wanna do it. So many of 'em are left alone 'cause their parents have to work or have other kids at home. Bein' able to care for 'em while givin' the mom, dad, or both the comfort of knowin' I'm there for their child brings me joy. I love kids and can't wait to have a few of my own," I admitted, making my plate.

"I hope the father won't be your current man. My grandchildren don't need to be caught up in that gene pool of craziness." I sighed at my mom's comment. "His whole family is slow as hell."

"Speaking of people with limited brain cells, did Jamal tell

21

you what he did on Friday?" I shook my head. "He decided he would piss in the bushes of a home that he was working at. The homeowner's daughter caught him. We were supposed to get more work from them after this project, but now, they decided to go with someone else. The only reason we got to complete this job was because I agreed to charge them half the price. It would cover the cost of the supplies and pay the guys, but there will be no profit for us."

The expression on my dad's face was one I hadn't seen in a long time. You could tell he was pissed by the way he slammed the mashed potatoes on his plate.

"Oh, no, I'm sorry, daddy."

"Princess, don't apologize for him. He's suspended for two weeks without pay. One more incident, and he's gone for good. I only tolerated his bullshit this far for you. Jamal is a waste of space. After pleading with me not to mention it to you because he wanted to tell you himself, his ass still didn't. I knew he wouldn't." My dad blew his breath. "Let's not let him ruin our evening and enjoy the meal your mom prepared for us."

I asked Jamal why he came home early on Friday. He expected me to be at work, but I had switched days with a coworker. His lying ass said they finished the job early, jumped in the shower, and was out the door. It would have been the perfect time for us to spend some quality time together. Since Jamal wanted to be dishonest, I planned on keeping his suspension to myself. If his ass left the house tomorrow morning, acting like he was going to work, I would be following him to see where he went.

Maybe it was time for me to finally open my eyes and see Jamal for who he really was. If I ended up alone, I'd just have to learn to be comfortable with myself.

* * *

"A'ight, Rain, I'm headin' out. I'll see you tonight."

Jamal kissed my forehead as I laid in the bed. He never mentioned the suspension, and neither did I. This nigga probably figured he was in the clear because normally I would bring up the smallest issue. If I never addressed something this big, Jamal probably figured my dad never mentioned it to me.

"Okay, babe, have a good day. I'll miss you," I lied.

As soon as I heard the door shut, I flung the covers back and jumped out of the bed. After throwing on some sweats and a hoodie, I slid on my black crocs and went to the front window. Once Jamal pulled out of the parking lot and drove off, I grabbed my phone and keys and exited the apartment. Harmony was already outside waiting for me with the engine running. We decided to take her car, since she just got a brand new one. This way Jamal wouldn't realize it was us on his tail.

"Whew, my nerves are so bad," I admitted, getting in the car and closing the door.

"And yo breath is foul as hell, damn."

Harmony used her free hand to cover her nose and mouth as she pulled off like a bat out of hell in pursuit of Jamal.

"Don't do me like that. I didn't have time to brush my teeth or wash my face," I mumbled, trying not to open my mouth all the way.

"Here, hang this on your ear."

This bitch handed me a Little Trees air freshener. I pulled my hoodie up over my face and laughed after throwing it at her.

"Give me some gum. I know you got 'bout seven packs of Fruit Stripe in here."

"It's in the middle console and don't eat the orange ones. Those my favorite," she informed me.

Harmony caught up to Jamal but made sure to stay two cars behind him. At first it appeared he was heading to his mom's house, but then he took a weird turn.

"Where the hell is he going?" I quizzed.

Jamal jumped onto the parkway, heading north.

"I don't know, but you givin' me gas and toll money 'cause fuck this shit. This raggedy ass nigga makin' me put miles on my new ride," Harmony complained. "And you better put his ass out after all of this. Ain't no man worth you goin' to jail."

"Who the hell is goin' to jail?" I questioned, confused.

"Yo ass after you bust his head to the white meat if he pulls up to another ho's house."

Harmony was definitely with the shits. She tried to run her last boyfriend over when she caught him cheating. If he didn't jump on the hood of her car, his ass would have been roadkill. Her crazy ass left tire tracks all over those people's freshly manicured lawn.

"If he is cheatin', she can have him. I'm not fightin' no one."

"Then why the fuck are we out here actin' like ghetto detectives?" Harmony spewed.

"I need proof so—"

"Girl, shut yo ass up." Harmony cut me off.

When we neared the next exit, she put her blinker on and drove toward it.

"Why are you gettin' off? Keep followin' him," I begged. "I need to see where he's goin'."

"Nope. I love you too much to let you watch this lowlife pull up to another woman's house to get his dick sucked while you sit in the car and cry. If you not gone get out, knock twice, then run up in that muthafucka like a bounty hunter to whip his ass while I stand guard, then there is no need for us to follow him. Yo gut already told you what this nigga is doin'. Seein' it won't change anythin' unless you plan on takin' action. Either keep dealin' wit' his lies and lettin' this ugly, pooh bear lookin' muthafucka play wit' the health of yo pussy, or choose you. At some point you have to put yourself first."

Tears began to fall as I listened to my best friend speak the truth. One thing Harmony didn't play about was me. We had been like sisters since the third grade. She never held back when it came to telling me the truth. Everyone needed someone in their life who would always tell them what they needed to hear and not what they wanted to hear. Harmony was that person for me.

"Thank you. I'm so glad I have you in my life."

"Stop fuckin' cryin' before I kill that bastard for you. He's not worth yo tears. I'm taking yo ass to the dollar store, so we can get some trash bags and dish liquid."

"Dish liquid?" I quizzed, wiping my face with the sleeve of my hoodie.

"Yeah, the bleach fucks wit' my asthma. The dish liquid makes the clothes and sneakers slimy and yields the same reaction from 'em." Harmony laughed.

I don't know what I would do without her.

Chapter Three

GRAY

"You over there deep in thought. Who has a hold of yo mind this early in the morning?" Bear quizzed.

He just picked me up from Gramps and Big Mama's house. Usually, I drove my own car, but when we had face-to-face meetings with our clients, we all rode together.

"Rain. I can't seem to get her outta my mind ever since our conversation yesterday. She stopped by after havin' dinner wit' her parents. We chilled in the basement for like an hour before she went on her way." I rested my head back on the seat.

"Her ass ain't neva gone let you hit, bruh. Rain has been on the radar of every muthafucka we know, and she chose Jamal's sorry ass. I don't know what type of voodoo dick that mutha-fucka got, but he has her on lock." Bear laughed.

"I ain't tryna just hit. I'mma make her mine. Rain not the

type of female you casually fuck for fun. She's the kind of woman you marry and build a legacy wit'. I need her to be my forever. And from what Rain told me, whateva hold he had on her is gone. That nigga on his way out, leavin' me the opportunity to claim what belonged to me in the first place."

As Bear navigated the streets, heading to Ant's house, I reflected back on my time spent with Rain.

"I almost didn't stop by." Rain smirked, talking shit when I opened the door to my basement apartment.

"Yeah, right, get cho slick talkin' ass up in here."

"Where's Ant," she quizzed as I closed the door.

"Kira kept blowin' his phone up, so he dipped off after his greedy ass ate two helpin's of Big Mama's peach cobbler."

Rain sighed after taking off her sneakers and making herself comfortable on the foot of my bed. I sat at the head of it, relaxing back on some pillows.

"My life isn't goin' the way I had it planned out in my head. All I wanted to do was live happily ever after, like in the fairytales. By now, I should have been married and pregnant with my second child. I wanted to have three kids, back-to-back, so they could grow up together."

"Well, you need a man first in order to do that," I joked.

Rain cut her eyes at me and pursed her lips.

"I know why my parents don't like Jamal, but you never told me yo reason for always talkin' shit 'bout him. What he do to you?" Rain questioned.

"You want the truth or for me to lie to you?" I quizzed.

"Have you ever lied to me before?" Rain sat up on her knees and looked me dead in the eyes.

"No..."

"So, don't start now." She tucked in her bottom lip, biting on it, looking sexy as hell.

Rain had dark brown eyes, chestnut skin tone, and shoulder length hair that she had pulled back into a ponytail. There was a twinkle in her eye whenever she smiled, and Rain always smelled edible. I wanted to take a bite out of her every time we crossed paths. Without a shadow of a doubt, this woman was top tier; gorgeous, intelligent, and loving.

The best part about this beauty was her heart. These days it was rare to come across someone who was genuine and would do anything for anyone without expecting anything back.

"He's usin' you. I'm not sayin' he neva loved or cared for you at some point. But from the outside lookin' in, Jamal knows he can have his cake and eat it too when it comes to you. That nigga in the streets like he a single man." I was honest with Rain.

"If you knew he was doin' me dirty, why wouldn't you tell me? We supposed to be betta than that." Rain's facial expression changed.

"Why would I tell you somethin' you already know? You wasn't gone do nothin' if I told you 'cause then you have to admit everyone was right 'bout him. I neva took you for the weak type, until you got wit' ol' boy. Somethin' in you changed. You won't let me all the way in, so I'm not privy to that information. And I'm not into hurtin' the people I care 'bout, so I stayed outta yo relationship." I shrugged my shoulders.

"I'm not weak!" Rain raised her voice.

"Yo, chill. You gettin' rowdy wit' the wrong one. I didn't hurt you... I'll neva hurt you if you were mine," I confessed.

Rain's face began to soften, and she actually cracked a smile.

"I know, Gray. But you and I can't go there, eva. You and Harmony are all I got, besides my parents. I can't risk our friendship."

"Then make me yo enemy, shit." She laughed.

I tapped my chest with two of my fingers, signaling Rain to lay her head on my heart like she always did when she was stressed. Her thick ass crawled over on my king size bed and snuggled up against me. Even though I wanted to strip her down and bury my face in between her legs, I never made any physical, sexual advances toward Rain.

Whenever the time came, I would allow her to make the first move. I never wanted to put Rain in a position where she felt pressured into doing something she wasn't ready to do.

"He lied straight to my face the other day. I gave Jamal all of me, and he took my kindness for weakness. Not only did he use me but my parents as well. They are completely done wit' him. I'm the only one still holdin' on for dear life. Why couldn't he be the man I needed him to be?"

"I can't answer that. The only man I can speak for is me. And I'm gonna always be here for you." I kissed the top of her head.

"Love you, Gray."

"I love you too, beautiful. Just say the word, and I'll end that nigga."

"Look at this crazy shit right here." Bear beeped the horn,

bringing me out of my private thoughts, and rolled down his window. "Why the fuck you out here in yo boxers?"

Ant was sitting on his front steps wearing nothing but some tight ass boxers. He made his way over to the truck.

"I'mma kill this bitch. She locked me outta my own damn house!"

"Why the fuck you got those fitted ass boxers on. You need to go up a few sizes, bruh." I laughed.

"It was the first thing I grabbed to put on after Kira tried to cut me while I was sleepin'. Her crazy ass went through my phone. I don't even know how she got in it 'cause I only use a passcode. This manic held a hatchet knife next to my dick and threatened to chop my shit off. I had to poke her in both eyes to get away. I've been sittin' out here for thirty minutes." Bear shook his head.

"We gone be late for this meetin' fuckin' wit' yo ass. You shoulda been dressed. Sleepin' in like we ain't got business to handle." I ran my hands down my face then sparked the blunt I was saving for later.

"Good pussy makes me go night night, and I ran into some after I left yo ass. That's the real reason Kira's mad. I didn't get in 'til three in the mornin'. She actually left me a plate of food on the stove wit' a note on it. The shit looked like a science project." Ant laughed. "I need y'all to come inside wit' me to get my phone and clothes. Her parents took our daughter wit' 'em, so she's in there alone, plottin'."

"You lucky I got my key on me." Bear killed the engine and hopped out of the car. "Gray, come on, bruh."

31

"She not 'bout to fuck up my high." I took another pull and blew the smoke out.

"Let me hit that." Ant reached for the blunt.

"Nah, you still got ass on yo lips. We both know you went straight to sleep when you got home, bypassin' the bathroom."

"Fuck you," Ant spewed.

I shrugged my shoulders and took another pull then put the blunt out. After getting out of the truck, we followed Ant back to his house. Bear unlocked the door and opened it.

"Well, if it ain't the doublemint twins and their sidekick." Kira had jokes, standing there looking like she was up to no good.

"Yo ass gettin' out today." Ant pointed his finger at her. "Start packin' yo shit right now."

"Nigga, you gone have to evict me. Accordin' to the law, I live here, and yo spineless ass can't just put me out. We in Jersey. They protect tenants."

Kira's eyes proved she had been up all night, or they were still red from when Ant poked them.

"Just go jump in the shower and get dressed, so we can go. You can deal wit' her simple ass later," Bear suggested.

"Who the fuck you callin' simple, Bear? You look like a bear, a grizzly. You wide back muthafucka."

"Keep talkin' shit." Bear rubbed his hands together.

"And I will. Fuck you and him. Y'all stuck wit' my ass for life 'cause I have yo niece. Since he don't wanna show me some respect, I'mma make his life a—"

Before she could finish her rant, Bear scooped Kira's ass up, threw her over his shoulder, and walked toward the front door. I followed them to see what he was going to do. Once he was outside, Bear made his way to the side of the house and tossed her ass into the blue recycling bin.

He rolled the bin to the top of the driveway, which was on a hill, leaned it back, and pushed the bin hard as hell. Kira screamed all the way down. Once she made it to the bottom, she crawled out like a wounded animal.

"I'm callin' the fuckin' police on yo ass, Bear." Kira started making her way back up the driveway, holding her head.

"Go 'head. I'mma tell 'em all I did was take out the trash. I told yo triflin' ass 'bout usin' my niece against us. Next time, I'll grant Ant full custody when I permanently silence you. Say one more thing."

Kira must have known Bear wasn't playing with her dirty ass because she immediately stopped talking.

"You gotta say no to drugs, Kira," I jeered while taking the blunt I put out earlier from behind my ear and blazing it back up.

"And make sure yo ass gone by the time we get back," Bear yelled over his shoulder.

A few minutes later, Ant made his way outside.

"Look at what she did to my phone." He showed us the battered iphone. "She beat it wit' a meat mallet. I hate her ass."

"Man, that's what you get for runnin' up in her ass raw. She been crazy." I finally passed him the blunt.

We walked over to Bear's truck and hopped in. I texted our

client to let her know we were running behind schedule due to a family emergency.

* * *

"Can you believe she wants us to steal a damn dog?" Ant hadn't stopped running his mouth since we walked out of the meeting. "We gotta draw the line somewhere."

"It's her dog too, so technically it's not stealin', and she's one of our best clients," I argued, making my way to the truck and getting in.

"We not a goddamn animal shelter. I don't even like dogs like that, which is why I got fish. She needs to call animal control and make up a lie and have 'em go get the dog," Ant continued.

"Shit, Goldie is willin' to pay us a grip to get that mutha-fucka, so I say we do it. It's probably one of the easiest jobs we had this year." Bear made his position known as he hopped in and started the engine.

"Well, we got to the end of the day to give her our decision. I knew Ant would have a problem wit' it, which was why I told her to let us ponder over it."

"Then Ant can stay the fuck home wit' Kira's dusty ass, and we'll split the money two ways," Bear suggested.

"Fuck both of y'all. She didn't even say what kind of dog it was, and when did we start gettin' involved in peoples' personal bullshit. This is between Goldie and her ex-husband." Ant laid down across the backseat.

"We got involved in yo personal bullshit when Kira had yo punk ass sittin' outside lookin' like an abandoned grown ass baby. All you needed was a big ass wicker basket to lay in and a note on yo chest. I shoulda called CPS and said I found a 312 month old on the front steps." Bear laughed.

"That shit ain't funny. I had no choice but to run outside before I had beans and no frank."

"You her lifeline. She not cuttin' shit off. If anythin', she gonna try and get pregnant again. Her crazy ass knows as long as she got yo kid, you gone hold her down. Allowin' her to stay wit' you was yo first mistake," I added.

"I only did that for my daughter. Y'all spermless niggas don't know nothin' 'bout that. But I now realize that was a mistake. And I ain't neva fuckin' her again."

"Lies..."

"Back to business. I say we do it. 100k just to pick up a dog named Buttercup. It will be the easiest money we ever made." Bear grinned.

"I agree. Ant, you in or you out? Either way, Bear and I are doin' it."

"I'm in. I need that to get Kira set up in her own shit. Wake me up when we pull up to my house."

Shaking my head, I relaxed back in my seat, glad I didn't have any baby momma drama.

Chapter Four

RAIN

"Why did you grab a cart? I thought we were just gettin' trash bags and dish liquid."

Harmony had a devilish grin on her face as she steered the little green cart through the craft aisle.

"I decided to go a step further. He's a bitch and needs to be treated as such."

"This is true. I can't help but wonder who she is, though. The worst part 'bout bein' cheated on is all the unknowns. Is she prettier than me? Does she even know I exist? What does he see in her that he didn't see in me? What did I do wrong? Why didn't he—"

"Stop it!" Harmony turned and faced me. "You did nothin' wrong. It's his loss. Who cares what she looks like or does wit' him. None of that shit matters. Knowin' all the answers to yo questions won't change the situation. Rain Ellington is a baddie. Hold yo head up and understand who the fuck you are."

I took a deep breath and nodded my head. Harmony was right. Losing me was the biggest mistake of Jamal's life.

"Maybe we should get some canned sardines to put in the bags." I smirked.

"That's what I'm talkin' 'bout! Focus on the matter at hand."

Harmony grabbed bottles of tacky glue and glitter then went over to the back wall and tossed five bottles of dish liquid in the cart. We headed over to the checkout after I grabbed the trash bags and a few other items I needed.

"Ugh, this ho." The cashier mumbled under breath as we approached her register, but we both heard her.

"Excuse you." I looked at her crazy.

"Not you, her." She pointed at Harmony.

"Just ring it up, stinky. And if you call me a ho again, I'll drag yo ass ova to the frozen food section and throw you up in there after I beat you in the face 'til yo eye cross," Harmony threatened, putting the items from the cart onto the conveyor belt.

"Stop givin' yo pussy out like free frosty coupons at Halloween time, and I won't have to call you outta yo name, ho," the cashier fired back, making me clutch my imaginary pearls.

"Listen, lake lizard, don't get mad at me 'cause yo pussy smell like pond piss. Neva approach the woman when yo man is the one who stepped out 'cause somethin' like this might happen."

The cashier didn't even get a chance to blink before Harmony leaned over and punched her in the mouth. Her head snapped back, but she didn't drop. This chick grabbed the handheld scanner and cracked Harmony in her forehead three times.

"Oh, damn." I couldn't believe how quick she reacted.

Harmony hopped over the counter, punched the woman again, and they got to rocking. It was like watching one of the viral fight videos on social media. The cashier wasn't no slouch and matched Harmony blow for blow. They were fighting so fast and hard, both of them fell into some boxes that were stacked in front of the store's window. Once the woman scorned ended up on top, I snatched her braids and pulled her ass off of my friend.

Harmony jumped up and grabbed a bunch of helium balloons that were floating above us. She wrapped them around the cashier's neck, then grabbed some more.

"No, friend, you gonna go to jail for murder."

I let go of the lady's hair and stopped Harmony.

"I'm not goin' to kill her. I just wanna make this bitch float away."

Some of the customers in the store were recording us while others were walking out without paying for their stuff.

"Let's go before they call the cops," I pleaded. "And you need to get yo inhaler. I can hear you wheezin'."

"I know, but I'm good. My body is used to me always fightin'."

By the time the manager came out of hiding, we were heading toward the exit with our items. I did leave a twenty dollar bill on the counter, though.

"I know where you live, ho. You'll see me again. Be ready to square up when you do."

The cashier was still talking shit. Most people didn't play in Harmony's face like that because she was known for whipping ass. They said people that fought all the time would one day meet their match, and Harmony definitely met hers today.

"What the fuck was that all about?" I quizzed.

"I'm fuckin' her man. Honestly, I didn't know he had a girl. The nigga lied." She shook her head.

"So, why you still dealin' wit' him? I'm just askin'."

Judging by the look Harmony gave me, she didn't appreciate my line of questioning. The fact that she continued to fuck this man after learning of his relationship status didn't sit well with me.

"I already sat on his face by the time I found out about her, and the dick is amazin'. The funny part is I planned on leavin' him alone. Now, I'm not." Harmony hit the button to unlock her doors but walked over to another car that was parked a few spaces from hers and keyed it. "Stupid, bitch. I'm gonna make her life a livin' hell."

"I'm guessin' that was her car," I stated, getting in the passenger seat.

"Yup." Harmony smiled and got in, starting the engine.

She grabbed her inhaler from her pocketbook and took a puff. After she took a couple of slow, deep breaths, I questioned her.

"Why didn't you tell me 'bout this guy?"

"Really?" Harmony shook her head and backed out of the spot. She put the car in drive and pulled off. "I knew you would have chastised me 'cause of what you were goin' through wit' Jamal. And I didn't wanna hear it, to be truthful."

I had confided in Harmony that I felt Jamal was being unfaithful when he started coming home late.

"True, but even though I might not agree wit' yo choices and will voice my opinion, you can still share yo life wit' me. I don't want us keepin' secrets. Look how you ended up fightin' in the dollar store while I stood there confused on how y'all even knew each other. And she almost whipped yo ass." I laughed.

"You had my back, though." Harmony smiled.

"And always will."

She put the music on, and we headed to my house. I couldn't believe this chapter of my life was coming to a close.

* * *

"Give me all his expensive sneakers."

Harmony had covered my kitchen table with a plastic table-cloth. I went into my bedroom and grabbed all the Jordans Jamal had in his collection.

"What are you 'bout to do?" I questioned.

"Bedazzle the hell out of 'em."

While she poured glue and sprinkled glitter on the sneakers, I went back into the room and started throwing Jamal's clothes into the trash bags. As I was cleaning out his dresser drawers, I found a picture of us. It was taken in a photobooth at a fair we went to three summers ago.

I rubbed my hand over the strip of pictures and let the tears trickle down my face. Jamal may have fallen out of love with me, but my heart was still all in. Even though I made the decision to finally throw in the towel on the one-sided relationship I had been in all these years, it wasn't easy to just cut off my feelings. When you spent ten years of your life loving someone, walking away was the last thing you wanted to do.

This man knew my deepest and darkest secret. He knew my body inside and out. Jamal was the only man who got to experience every part of me, and I didn't know if I was capable of letting someone else in that way again. To trust someone with my heart after it had been betrayed wasn't something I was looking forward to.

After wiping away the evidence of my pain, I continued on with the task at hand. Each time I put some items in the trash bag, I squirted dish liquid all over them. Once the bag was full, I emptied a can of sardines into it.

"This some funky ass shit," I complained, dragging the bags to the front door.

"I'm almost done here. We can start bagging these up."

"Jamal might try to fight my ass after he sees this shit." I kissed my teeth.

Harmony had those sneakers looking like ten fairies threw up on them. They went from Jordans to My Little Pony.

"He ain't crazy. Gray would have that muthafucka floatin' in the Navesink River by the end of the night. That man don't play 'bout you. You know once the bill collector finds out you single, single, he gone be on yo ass even harder." Harmony grinned.

"Believe me, I know. If I could do it all over again, I woulda definitely have chosen Gray. But that ship has sailed. None of the friends to lovers relationships I know of worked out. You don't really know someone 'til you live wit' 'em. And that goes for all relationships."

I finished bringing the bags from the bedroom to the front door, then bagged up the sneakers with Harmony.

"A'ight. Let's take this shit outside and sit it on the curb, this way he has no reason to come in here at all," Harmony suggested.

"Yes, and I just called an emergency locksmith to change my locks. It's gonna cost me, but I can sleep peacefully knowin' he can't just walk in."

I opened the door and dragged two bags out. When I got to the end of my walkway, Jamal pulled up. Harmony was right behind me with a bag in each of her hands.

"Don't panic. Just sit the bags down and go back into the house." Harmony spoke in a calm tone.

"What the fuck are you two doin'?" Jamal quizzed, getting out of his car.

"Takin' out the trash." I spun on my heels and walked fast as hell back to the house.

"I think you might wanna get back in your car." Harmony tried to keep Jamal from coming inside the house.

"And I think you might wanna find some business of yo own to tend to 'cause this ain't it." He pushed her out of the way.

"Don't put cho fuckin' hands on me, nigga." Harmony pushed him back.

"You're not comin' in here." I stood in front of the doorway, blocking him. "All yo shit is packed up and—"

Jamal snatched me up by my shirt, pushing his way inside while dragging me along. He threw me onto the couch then walked into the bedroom.

"Where the fuck is all my shit!" he yelled. "They betta not be in those trash bags."

This enraged psycho tore one of the bags open and pulled out a sparkly Jordan.

"You get what you give. Yo ass wasn't at work 'cause you're suspended. And we followed you." Jamal's eyes turned into slits when I said that. "Yeah, the bitch you fuckin' lives up north, huh?"

"Oh, okay, so your jealousy and insecurities got the best of you today. Now, you wanna throw us away. I'm the only nigga that's gone deal wit' yo crazy ass, and you gone replace everythin' you fucked up."

"Say whateva you want. I don't care anymore. You were my biggest lesson, and I'm not replacin' shit."

"Get the fuck out before I slice yo ass open."

I didn't even see Harmony go into the kitchen and get a knife. She was holding it like she was ready to filet his ass.

"Wow, you movin' like that, Harmony? I hope you're here for yo friend when she ends up splittin' in half. You know she can't handle stress well. Fuck both you stank ass bitches." Jamal spat at us.

"Spittin' just like the humpback camel you are." I shook my head in disgust.

"Bye, Heathcliff. And I'm referrin' to the fat, orange cat not Dr. Huxtable, you wide back bastard."

Harmony followed behind him with the knife, making sure he left.

"I'm gonna stay at my parent's house tonight. I don't trust him," I shared.

"Yeah, me neither. There was nothin' but darkness in his eyes. He's not gonna walk away quietly."

Harmony and I waited for Jamal to drive away before sitting the rest of the bags outside. Once the locksmith came and changed the locks, we left. My parents would definitely be happy to know Jamal and I are over, but once they find out under what circumstances and that he put his hands on me, all hell was going to break loose.

Chapter Five

GRAY

"Yeah, we all here. What's good?"

I had Goldie on speaker phone. Bear and Ant stayed at my beach house last night, which was located along the Jersey Shore, since we knew we would be heading out to do this job. We just didn't know the time. From May to September, this was my home away from home. During the other months, I resided on my compound in Upper Freehold. The area was secluded and out of the way.

"Okay, I saw on Facebook he just left for a meeting in south Jersey. The fact that he posted his every move on social media was one of the things I hated about him. In our line of business, it allowed your enemies to know your every move, which was one of the reasons I left his ugly ass. You guys should have plenty of time to get in and snatch up my lil Buttercup before he returns."

"Aight, I'll hit you back once we're in route to you." I ended the call.

Normally, we all drove our own vehicles to a job, but since we were picking up a dog, it was best we rode together.

"I'll drive," Bear informed us.

Whenever we were together, his ass always wanted to drive.

"So, I gotta sit in the back wit' the dog. Y'all betta have a cage for that muthafucka." Ant hopped up from the table we were sitting at and headed for the bathroom.

"Shit, we need a cage for yo ass, real talk." I laughed.

"I heard that, Grayson," Ant yelled, trying to be funny by saying my whole first name.

After we got our shit together, we headed out. Most of the day was already gone, so I wanted to go and get back. I had Bear stop at the local pet shop to grab a medium size cage and a couple chew toys before we jumped on the parkway.

Since Goldie used to live in this home and set the security system up herself, she was able to provide us with the broadcast frequency that I sent over to my tech guy. He provided us with the correct wireless camera jammer that would prevent her ex-husband from receiving an alert from the security system by disabling it, which also allowed us to enter the home without being recorded.

"I know I agreed to come, but I still feel like this is a bad idea. When somethin' seems too easy, it's usually a catch to it." Ant sighed. "We collect money, not animals."

"You scared of a fuckin' ankle biter? Sit back and don't say shit else the rest of the ride. Matter of fact, make yo'self useful by rollin' up."

Bear reached inside the console in between our seats and tossed a bag of weed and a couple Backwoods at Ant.

"I'mma roll up, but I'm not gone shut up."

We had to listen to Ant talk shit all the way to our destination. With the jammer activated, Bear pulled up to the house that was more like a mini mansion sitting on a few acres of land that was masterfully manicured. The driveway was about a quarter of a mile long and wrapped around the house, so we parked in the back.

Goldie said there was a side door that was a part of the original construction of the house that her ex refused to upgrade during their remodel because he liked the look of it. She said it could be picked open with the right tools. I learned to pick locks at the age of ten for fun.

With my gloves on and tools handy, I gained entry into the house. The door led us into a small area that looked like they used it to house their coats and shoes if they came in this way.

"A'ight, lets locate this lil pup and get the hell up outta here. He must be upstairs 'cause I don't hear no yappin'," I informed them.

We headed out of the room and walked into the kitchen. Everything in it was hi-tech. The fridge had a touch screen on it, and all the appliances were controlled by motion sensors.

"This too much house for one damn person. He probably don't even cook. Shit looks untouched." Ant shook his head.

As we made our way out of the kitchen and down a long hallway, I suggested we separate and quietly search the rooms and meet back up toward the front of the house.

"Maybe he took it wit' him 'cause I don't hear or see a damn dog." Bear sighed.

We were standing at the bottom of this massive staircase that was the centerpiece of the home. All of a sudden, the sound of a low growl caught our attention. When I looked up to see where it was coming from, a big ass Cane Corso was staring down at us from the top of the stairs. He looked to be about 100 pounds.

"Ankle biter did you say? That's a muthafuckin' body biter. I'm out."

Ant took off running, causing the dog to charge us at full speed. By the time we made it to the kitchen, he was on our heels, forcing us to jump on top of the extra large island.

"This all yo fault," I yelled at Ant. "If you would have remained calm, we could have backed out slowly and had a decent head start."

"Nigga, we black. Run first and figure shit out lata is what we do. I wasn't waitin' 'round for yo exit plan," Ant defended.

"Okay, genius, what are we gone do now?" Bear quizzed.

The Cane Corso was barking and jumping at us, making thick globs of slob fly out his mouth.

"I don't know what we gone do, but Buttercup ain't gone fit in the cage y'all got. I know that." Ant laughed. "I got some edibles for him. That should calm his ass down."

"We can't give the dog weed. And it would take too long to

take effect anyway. We need to distract his ass, so I can get to the truck. I picked up some melatonin the other day and left 'em in there. Dogs can take it. It sedates 'em naturally," Bear explained.

"I see someone has been watchin' *Animal Planet*," Ant joked.

"A'ight, Ant, you and I will make a run for it, making him chase us. This way Bear can sneak out the back."

"Nigga, is you crazy. He almost caught us the first time." Ant ran his hands down his face.

"That's the only way. Otherwise, we gone still be sittin' here when his master gets back and calls the boys on our asses. You wanna go to jail for breakin' and enterin' or get chased by a Cane Corso?" I quizzed.

"I knew I shoulda stayed my black ass at home. Fuck, man! I rather deal wit' Kira than this bullshit. A'ight."

"Bear, do somethin' to get him to go ova to yo side, so Ant and I can make a run for it. We gone run to the front of the house and around the staircase then back to the kitchen."

This nigga started barking like he was a damn dog. It worked because Buttercup went around to where Bear was crouched down at and started barking back.

"Now, Ant, go!" I yelled.

We hopped off the island and took off. Buttercup gave chase. Ant was in front, leading the way. I never ran so fast in my life. When we rounded the staircase, I took the lead.

"Help! Help me, Gray. I'm 'bout to die. I don't wanna go out like this." Ant screamed in a high pitched voice, sounding like a bitch. "This nigga got me. Good doggy, Buttercup, good doggy."

When I stopped and looked back, Ant was on the ground and Buttercup had his pants leg in his mouth, dragging him. I ran over and scooped him up by his underarms. Now, it was a tug-of-war between me and Buttercup for possession of Ant.

I pulled as hard as I could, walking backwards. Buttercup wasn't giving up.

"Ant, kick yo sneakers off."

"What is that gone do?" he questioned.

"Just do it, damn."

Ant managed to come out of his sneakers, but Buttercup still had a death grip on his jeans, slobbing and growling.

"Unbuckle yo pants and grab yo boxers. When I pull again, yo jeans are gonna come off, and we out."

"You sure this gone work? Don't let this muthafucka bite my dick off, bruh." Ant was nervous as hell.

"On the count of three. 1, 2, 3."

I pulled as hard as I could, and Ant slid out of his jeans like a snake. We ran fast as hell to the kitchen. I jumped back on the island first, at the same time Bear was hopping on. Ant came sliding in on his slippery ass socks, crashing into the island. We pulled him up just in time.

"What the hell happened to you?" Bear busted out laughing.

"I tripped and fell, and Buttercup got me. If Gray didn't come back for me, you wouldn't be a twin anymore."

"Just stop talkin', Ant. You sound crazier than you look

right now." I shook my head. "Bear, throw the pills at him. Hopefully, he eats the shits."

Bear tossed four tablets on the floor, and Buttercup licked them up.

"If he don't die, he gone be paralyzed. Four? Yo ass weigh more than him. Would you take four damn pills?" Ant stared at his brother.

"No, but I'm not a damn dog. We need his ass to go to sleep fast."

"What's the dosage on the bottle?" I quizzed.

"Umm, five mg," Bear answered.

"Yeah, Ant might be right this time."

Buttercup eventually stopped barking at us. Thirty minutes later, his ass was knocked out. After Ant got dressed, we carried Buttercup to the truck and laid him in the trunk. I called Goldie to let her know we were on our way.

"You guys must have my Buttercup," she cooed.

"Yeah, but you failed to mention Buttercup wasn't so damn lil," I spewed.

"He's still a baby, only ten months. Maybe I could have given you a heads up, but that would have taken the element of surprise out of it. I hope he didn't cause too much trouble." Goldie knew her ass was wrong.

"Nah, we just had to give him somethin' to calm down. He should be awake in 'bout four hours."

She gasped, and I disconnected the call.

On the way back home, I got a 911 text from Rain, but it was from her mom, which was odd. She asked me to stop by the house and not to text back, stating Rain had no idea she was contacting me. We just pulled up.

"Y'all can leave me here. I'll find my way home."

"I think I fractured my hip when I crashed into that island. Goldie owes us more than an extra 25k," Ant sneered.

"If it's fine wit' Bear, you can keep the extra money. You did take a beatin'." I laughed and hopped out.

Before going over to the Ellingtons, I stopped by to say hello to Gramps and Big Mama. Gramps yelled at me on the Ring camera that they were busy and to get the hell on. All I could do was smile. For them to be seventy and still going at it gave me hope for me and my future wife.

I approached the Ellingtons' door and knocked on it. Rain answered with a shocked expression on her face.

"What are you doin' here?"

"Yo mom invited me." Her eyes got wide.

"Don't be rude, dear. Let him in." Mrs. Ellington spoke.

Rain appeared visibly upset. I don't know what I was walking into, but it was apparent she wasn't happy to see me.

Chapter Six

RAIN

"How and why?" I folded my arms across my chest and glared at my mom as we gathered in the family room.

"I texted him from your phone then deleted it, so you wouldn't know. If I didn't, you would have tried to stay mute about what happened. Gray is the only one who can help with this situation. He would have found out eventually."

"Find out and help wit' what?" Gray quizzed.

"You had no right goin' behind my back. This is my business, and I can handle it myself. Gray bein' involved will only make it worse," I explained. "If I wanted him to know, I woulda told him myself."

"Someone needs to tell me what the hell is goin' on." Gray looked back and forth between my mom and I.

"Jamal put his hands on Rain. She stayed here last night, scared he would come back to the house while she was sleeping and hurt her." My mom tightened her lips. "I started to call the police, but they would have just told her to sign a restraining order, like a piece of paper will stop him. He needs to be handled in a way only you can do."

Gray immediately became enraged. He was trying his hardest to keep his emotions in check, but by the way he clenched his fist, furrowed his brow, and blew his breath, Gray wasn't doing a good job.

"Why didn't you call me last night when that muthafucka put his hands on you?" Gray questioned. "Excuse my language, Miss Deb."

He never took his eyes off me when addressing my mom.

"Because the way you handle things scares me. I know what you are capable of, especially when it comes to me." I spoke honestly. "And he only snatched me up and threw me on the couch. Jamal neva actually hit me."

"See, she keeps making excuses for his behavior. Blaming herself because she finally came to her senses and put his ass out." My mom threw her hands in the air and started pacing back and forth. "Her father is ready to kill him. I keep checking his location, making sure he's still at work and not out looking for Jamal."

"Y'all can leave the killin' to me." The look in Gray's eyes told me he meant every word he just spoke.

"This is exactly why I didn't want you to know." My voice cracked.

"And Gray's response is exactly why I wanted him to know. That bastard put his hands on the wrong one. I don't care if it was just a snatch and a push, the results were the same as if he punched you in the face." Sadness consumed my mom's face. "Rain, you can try to downplay it all you want, but I know when my child is terrified. You were trembling when you walked in the door last night. I saw the fear in your eyes. Tell Gray how you called your job and told them you were sick because you think he might show up there."

"What!" Gray spun on his heels and headed for the front door.

"Stop, Gray!" I yelled, chasing behind him. "Please, don't walk out that door. If something happens to you, I would neva forgive myself."

He stopped and turned around to face me. The expression he wore was one of confusion.

"If something happens to me? Do you not know who the fuck I am, like for real?"

"I know exactly who Grayson Deeds is and didn't mean it the way you're takin' it. I don't want you to have blood on yo hands ova my bullshit." I hung my head.

He placed his hand under my chin and lifted my face up toward his.

"I'd die for you, Rain Ellington." A lump formed in my throat. "No one, and I mean no one puts their hands on you and continues to breathe the same air as you."

"Listen, I know there's nothin' I can say to stop you from goin' after Jamal. All I ask is that you don't end his life. I don't want that on my conscience. Okay?" Gray nodded, removing his hand.

"Why can't I tell this beautiful face no?"

He smiled then tucked in his bottom lip, biting on it, and sighed. This man was fine.

"Because you love me," I cooed. "And you're my best friend."

"Both are true."

"I need y'all to stop playing and get together already, so I can live happily ever after."

We didn't realize my mom was even standing there the entire time.

"Mom, really." I shook my head.

"Miss Deb, you and I are on the same page." Gray grinned. "Can y'all excuse me for a moment. I need to step outside and make some calls. And Rain, can you drop me off at home? I don't have my car."

"Yes, she can." I frowned at my mom for answering for me. "What? You ain't doing nothing." My mom shrugged her shoulders.

Gray walked out the door and closed it behind him.

"Why would you say yes? He coulda caught an Uber or somethin'. I'm not emotionally prepared to be around people right now."

"Gray isn't people, and you like him. I can see it in your eyes when you look at him." My mom smiled.

"I'm conflicted when it comes to Gray. He might not be

able to handle who I really am. Our friendship means more to me than a relationship."

"So, you never told him about Storm?" my mom questioned.

"No... I could never find the right time." I fought back the tears that threatened to fall.

"Awe, my sweet girl. That explains a lot. You settled for Jamal because he was there for you during one of your darkest moments. Were you afraid Gray would see you differently if he found out?" I nodded my head. "Gray isn't just any guy. He's the one. Why do you think he's still single? I never saw him bring a girl home. You're the only one who spends time with him and his grandparents. They adore you."

"Umm, 'cause we've been their neighbor my entire life."

"And they feel like I do when it comes to you and Gray being a couple, and so does your dad. We've already planned the wedding. All we needed was Jamal out of the way. Don't mess up what the universe has placed before you. Divine timing never misses."

"Okay, mom, I hear you." I just wanted her to be quiet.

"Alright, this is the last thing I'm going to say. One day he's going to move on. Do you think your heart would be able to watch your best friend marry another woman? Have kids with her? Live the life that was yours because you were too afraid to seize the moment—"

"You said one last thing."

Gray walked back in just in time.

"Sorry 'bout that. You ready, beautiful?"

"Yeah, let me grab my keys," I answered.

"Will you be home for dinner?" my mom asked, being annoying, as Gray and I made our way out the door.

I didn't even bother to answer, but I saw Gray shake his head at her from the corner of my eye.

"This is my first time in your beach house. I love it."

"Hopefully, it's not the last. You can kick yo shoes off and make yo'self at home. The bathroom is down the hall on your left if you need to freshen up."

I excused myself to go wash my hands and throw some water on my face. Gray wouldn't allow me to just drop him off. He begged me to have dinner with him; something we haven't done in a minute. Before I got with Jamal, Gray and I had dinner at least twice a week. He'd be at my house, or I'd go over to his and chill with him, Big Mama, and Gramps.

My mom's parents died in a house fire when I was sixteen, and my dad's parents lived out of state, so Big Mama and Gramps became surrogate grandparents to me over the last ten years, even though they always considered me a part of the family.

"You good?" Gray quizzed when I returned.

"Yes, thank you."

"Follow me into the kitchen. I'mma 'bout to make us a drink to sip on while we wait for the chinese food I ordered to get here," he instructed.

"Dag, you didn't even ask me what I wanted, big head." He laughed.

"Beef and broccoli with an order of chicken wings fried hard," Gray responded.

"And..." I smirked.

"Extra duck sauce, and I asked them to replace the white rice with shrimp fried rice."

"You still remember." I grabbed a seat on one of the barstools.

He had a whole bar setup, like one you would find in a restaurant or actual bar. Gray walked around the counter. The wall behind him was mirrored, giving you a beautiful view of the state of the art kitchen in the background.

"I'll neva forget."

Gray made us a Long Island iced tea. It was the first drink we shared together on each of our twenty-first birthdays, which happened to be a week apart.

"Whew... damn. How long did you leave it in Long Island? This shit strong as hell." I cleared my throat after taking a sip.

"You ain't gone do nothin' but babysit it anyway. By the time the ice melts, it'll be perfect. Grab it and let's go relax in the living room. You can choose the movie." Gray led the way.

The floor to ceiling windows gave a panoramic view of the shoreline as we made our way through the house.

"I wanna watch somethin' funny, like *Norbit*."

"Yeah, my TV don't play that. Choose another one." Gray laughed.

He pointed for me to take a seat on the oversized couch.

There was a section in the middle of it for our drinks. After I sat down, I sipped my drink and placed it in the cup holder. Gray passed me his cup to sit down and grabbed a blanket from the stack that was piled up neatly in the corner of the room and threw it at me.

I caught it then patted the empty space next to me. Gray came over and sat next to me. The couch was so big, it looked like we were sitting up in a bed.

"How 'bout *Brown Sugar*." I suggested another movie. "My mom and dad used to watch it all the time. It's a romantic comedy 'bout two best friends who are both in their own relationships, but realize they were meant to be together."

"Oh, so they made a movie 'bout us?"

"Whateva, bruh." I smiled.

While Gray searched for the movie, I spread the blanket over us. It felt good to spend time alone with him and it not be a Sunday.

About ten minutes after he found the movie and started it, Gray got an alert on his phone that the food had arrived.

"I'll be right back. Keep my seat warm."

Yo seat ain't the only thing that's warm.

I paused the movie, so he didn't miss any of it. Gray returned a few minutes later with our food on a wooden tray with handles. We ate until we were full then he took everything away after giving me a warm rag to clean my hands. All the ice had melted in my drink, so I took a few more sips. It was perfect, just like Gray said it would be.

We cuddled and watched the rest of the movie. Once it was

over, Gray hopped up and took his shirt off, revealing his chiseled body that was covered in tattoos. Even though it wasn't the first time I had seen him shirtless, it was the first time my body reacted to it.

"I'm 'bout to take a shower, care to join me." His request caught me off guard.

I was already distracted by his visually tantalizing physique.

"Are you serious right now?"

"I'm not here to play no games wit' you, Rain. I know exactly what I want, and it's you. It's always been you. Yeah, I have someone I fuck wit' sexually, but that's the extent of our situationship. There's no emotional connection. I'm in and I'm out, literally. But that's all over wit', now that you are here. The only woman who has ever had my heart is you. I've just been waiting for you to finally claim it," Gray expressed.

"What if it doesn't work out? We could end up hatin' each other. I don't know if I'm willin' to take that chance."

"It's a chance I'm willin' to take. You kept usin' that shitty ass relationship you were in as an excuse. It's ova. Then you wanna hide behind our friendship, which is stupid as hell 'cause the fact that we are friends can only help us. Tell me the truth, Rain. What's the real reason you are afraid to take the next step wit' me?"

I took a deep breath and stared into Gray's alluring, brown eyes.

"There's a side to me you don't know. A side I'm not ready to share wit' you yet. You deserve to be wit' someone who isn't as complicated as I am. I'm broken, Gray... I'm broken." Tears streamed down my face.

He held his hands out for me to grab and pulled me up and off the couch. Gray kissed me as he held my body close to his. It was soft and sensual, making me feel tingly all over. When our lips parted, he whispered in my ear.

"Let me fix you."

Before I could respond, Gray picked my thick ass up, and I instinctively wrapped my legs around his waist. He carried me up the steps and into his master bedroom.

It's 'bout to happen. It's really 'bout to happen. Pussy don't fail me now.

Chapter Seven

GRAY

I put Rain down once we made it to the master bedroom. She stood in front of me as I sat on the bed. The way her eyes searched my face let me know I wasn't the only one excited about this moment.

"Since this is our first time, I'mma be a gentleman tonight and let Grayson have control. We'll ease into it and go at yo pace. Now, tomorrow mornin', Gray is gonna show back up. He's unhinged and doesn't hold back at all. Just know you will always have the power to choose who makes you cum. And it doesn't matter who's in the driver's seat, you will arrive at yo destination each and every time. The only thing that changes is the manner in which you get there."

Rain hung onto every word I spoke. She let out a soft moan

when I finished talking. I pulled her closer to me and unbuttoned her jeans then unzipped them.

"Take 'em off," I instructed Rain.

She slowly slid the jeans down over her wide hips to her ankles. Rain stepped out of them after placing her hands on my shoulders for leverage.

"Remove yo shirt."

Watching her undress in front of me was something I fantasized about often. Rain's body was perfect. She was built like a brickhouse, just how I liked it.

"Take everything else off." Rain did as she was told. "You look beautiful."

I leaned forward and kissed her stomach. After admiring the nakedness in front of me some more, I stood up and removed all my clothing. Rain's eyes immediately focused on my dick. When she licked her lips, I knew she approved.

Grabbing Rain by the hand, I led her to the bathroom and into the shower, which took up a huge portion of my master bath. I started the water, and once the right temperature was reached, I placed Rain underneath it. She let her head fall back as the water saturated her body.

I lathered her from head to toe then myself. We rinsed off and got out. Before heading back into the bedroom, I removed two towels from the warmer. When I draped one over Rain's shoulders she smiled, then I wrapped the other around my waist and secured it.

"You're spoilin' me already," Rain cooed as I dried her off.

"This is nothin'." I smiled. "From here on out, it's my

mission to make you feel special each and every day, startin' now. Get in the middle of the bed and lay on yo back."

I tossed the decorative pillows onto the floor and pulled the cover back"

"Whew... I can't believe we really doin' this," Rain said, getting on the bed.

It felt like there was a slight hesitation in her voice.

"Like I said, at yo pace. If you not fully committed and wanna wait longer, we can. I don't want you to feel any pressure or think if you change yo mind I might get it somewhere else. I'm yours and yo ass is mine. From here on out it's us," I clarified.

She sat up on her elbows.

"I'm good. I was just thinkin' out loud. Believe me, I want this as much as you do. Maybe even more. You have always been the one, Grayson. Do as you please wit' me."

Rain laid back, spreading her legs apart. I climbed in between them and kissed her lips before taking a taste. Her pussy was fat and juicy, making my dick throb.

"Ahhh." She was moaning already, and I was just getting started.

The more I licked and sucked, the wetter Rain became. I had to hold her legs open by pressing on her knees because she kept trying to clamp down on my head. When I flickered my tongue back and forth over her clit, I could feel her body shake.

"You a'ight?" I questioned, smirking.

"Mmmmm, yes. It feels so good."

I went back to devouring Rain's pussy, coating my tongue

with her nectar. When I slid a finger inside her opening, it was tight but gushy. Imagining my dick in its place aroused me even more. Inserting another finger made Rain moan out in ecstasy.

"How does that feel?" I watched her arch her back when my thumb caressed her clit as my fingers searched for her G-spot.

Rain didn't answer, she massaged her titties instead, pinching her nipples. Watching her made my dick brick hard. It was time to make her cum for the first time.

I kept rubbing until I saw her body tense up and her mouth open, like her words were caught in her throat. With my fingers on the right location, I went back to sucking on Rain's clit, bringing her into a full body spasm.

"Oooooh, yes, Grayson, right there."

Once she was done, Rain relaxed her legs. I watched as she took a few deep breaths and shook her head. Getting up, I went and grabbed a condom.

"How you want it?" I quizzed, stroking my dick.

"From the side, then we can finish wit' me on top." She licked her lips.

Rain rolled over to the right, keeping her bottom leg straight while sliding the top one up, looking like a flamingo that fell down while standing on one leg.

I positioned myself behind her, rubbing her ass cheek before lifting it up and sliding inside that tight, wet pussy.

"Sssssss, shit." It felt like Rain's pussy gave me a welcome home hug.

Closing my eyes and biting down on my lip, I had to remain still to gather myself before I came prematurely. Jamal fumbling

Rain was nasty work, but stepping out to go get takeout when there was a Michelin Star culinary delight waiting for you at home was diabolical.

This pussy was a ten out of ten, and I definitely recommend Rain not to ever try me. I'd rather end her life before I allowed anyone else to experience what now belonged to me.

Till death do we part, and we ain't even married.

As I started thrusting in and out of Rain, she moaned out loud and rubbed on her clit. I placed my hand over hers, so we could play in the pussy together. Her juices dripped all over our fingers. When Rain pulled her fingers away and placed them in my mouth, so I could taste her again, it almost made me bust. I had to pull out and tell her to get on top.

Who knew she was this nasty?

I laid on my back while Rain positioned herself over me with one knee down and the other one up. She grabbed my dick and lined it up with her opening. Once Rain put the head in, she put her other knee down, allowing her pussy to swallow my dick whole.

"Goddamn," I let out, grabbing her ass.

"You ready to drown?" Rain questioned, staring into my eyes.

"Like a body weighed down wit' an anchor in the middle of the ocean," I replied.

Rain started off slow, rocking back and forth while squeezing her titties together and licking her nipples. They were hard like pebbles, and I wanted to suck on them myself. Her hips and ass rippled as Rain picked up her speed. She made my dick move around like the controller on Ms. Pac-Man when someone was trying to get away from the red ghost.

It was all about Rain right now, so I let her stay in control by not fucking her back. Watching her expressions change as she tried to snatch my soul was pleasurable enough.

"Ahhhh, I'mma 'bout to cum. It's right there," Rain uttered.

She leaned forward and grabbed my shoulders. Rain wasn't holding back. With her titties in my face, she doubled down by clenching her walls around my dick and thrusting her pussy forward. This was the first time a woman laid on top of me and basically fucked my ass. I loved it.

"Shit, you 'bout to make me bust," I confessed.

"Uhhhhh!" Rain's body began to jerk as she kept on thrusting.

I released once I knew she had. When Rain collapsed on my chest, I kissed her forehead and rubbed her back. She remained motionless until my dick lost its blood flow. Rain climbed off of me and laid on her back.

"That was everythin' I thought it would be... and more. Thank you."

"For what?" Rain laughed.

"For trustin' me wit' yo heart." I looked over at her.

As she stared at the ceiling, I could see Rain's eyes tear up.

"Thank you for waitin'.

"Mmmmm, mmmmmm, mmmmm."

Hearing Rain moan while I was fucking the shit out of her from behind was music to my ears. I slammed into her over and over again while she was on all fours, taking it like a champ.

We fell asleep last night with her wrapped in my arms. She was up before me and had hopped in the shower. Once I got in and out, Rain had on my robe, collecting her clothes. Her ass must have forgotten I told her Gray would show up in the morning.

When she asked me where the laundry room was I grabbed her clothes, threw them back on the floor, then tossed her solid ass on the bed. Snatching the robe off of Rain, I buried my face in her pussy and devoured it, along with her ass.

Before she knew it, I had Rain folded up like origami. She was turned every which way but loose as I made her cum over and over again.

"I'mma fuck yo ass 'til you lose the ability to verbally communicate. The only way you gone be able to tell me how good this dick feels is through sign language."

I snatched Rain's head back by her hair and kissed her. She matched my energy and kissed me back just as hard. It was wet and sloppy as our tongues fought for control. Releasing her hair, I went back to pounding away.

Slowing down, I watched as my dick slid in and out of Rain's pussy. The sounds coming from it being so wet excited me, causing me to increase my stroke. I pushed Rain's head down into the bed and grabbed her hips. The only noise that could be heard now was the slapping of our skin as my pelvic area connected against her ass.

I was in beast mode and showed her no mercy. Rain clenched the fitted sheet so hard she pulled it off the bed. She looked back at me and bit down on her lip, letting her eyes speak for her. They were filled with lust. Obviously, Rain enjoyed the pleasurable pain I was delivering.

My dick reacted to the sexiness of the look she gave me. I erupted as my body tensed up then convulsed. Immediately after I flipped Rain over and ate her pussy. She squirmed and tried to get away, but I held onto her massive thighs while viciously licking her clit. By the time I was done my face looked like a glazed donut, and Rain was sprawled out, panting.

"Well, good mornin' to you too, Mr. Gray." We both laughed.

Chapter Eight

"Why can't you just wait for me to take you ova there?" Gray quizzed. "I have somethin' to handle wit Ant and Bear, then we can go afterwards."

We were in the bathroom. Gray was posted up against the sink while I stood in front of him.

"Harmony is gonna meet me there, so I won't be alone. All I wanna do is grab a few of my things. Yo ass has been holdin' me hostage. Shit, I need some fresh air." I shook my head.

I had been at Gray's home for the last three days, fucking and eating. He had a private chef come over to cook us the most amazing meals. Each morning we had a hot breakfast waiting for us when we came downstairs, then the chef would prepare lunch and dinner and leave, only to return and repeat the next day.

"If you need some fresh air, stick yo head outta one of these damn windows." I cut my eyes at Gray.

"Whateva, bruh. Those panties you got are too small, and they end up a g-string two seconds after I put 'em on. The bras are titty corsets. I was only able to fit the sleep shirts."

Gray was a sweetheart and had some items delivered to the house for me, but the sizing was off.

"I wrote you were a plus size beauty in the notes, shit," Gray defended.

"And I love you for that. It's not yo fault. Whoever went shoppin' obviously doesn't know what plus size means." I licked his lips then kissed him.

"Don't start nothin' yo ass can't finish. I'll have you bent over, grabbing yo ankles while I bust yo ass. Keep playin'." I smiled and removed the sleep shirt I had on, exposing my nakedness.

Gray spun me around and grabbed my pussy while sucking on my neck. He squeezed and manhandled it before inserting two fingers inside my wetness. When his fingers fondled my clit, I moaned out loud. As promised, Gray had me grab my ankles and fucked me until my knees buckled.

We ended up on the floor, with me riding him reverse cowgirl. He released within minutes after I leaned forward with my hands on his knees and went crazy on his ass, making his toes grip the air.

"A'ight." I got up and caught my breath before talking

again. "I'mma shower and get on up outta here before Harmony starts blowin' up my phone. I'll call you before I come back ova to make sure yo ass is here. My mom wants me to stop by. She said a package came to her house for me this mornin'."

I stepped inside the shower and turned on the water. He joined me. Afterwards, I got dressed and put back on the clothes I originally wore there. Gray washed them for me and had my stuff smelling like fabric softener, just the way I liked it.

Kissing him goodbye, I exited the beach house and hopped into my car. On the drive over to my house I thought about how different my life was going to be, now that I had a real man by my side. When it came to Jamal and Gray, they were night and day. Jamal was all I knew sexually, so I had nothing to compare him to. Now that I experienced Grayson and Gray, I could never go back.

That man had me crawling the walls. There was a freaky side to Gray that was an unexpected surprise. He sprinkled pop rock candy around my areolas and licked it off. Before I gave him head, he placed a Listerine strip on my tongue, advising me to let it melt before I got to slurping. I was blindfolded as Gray traced my body with ice cubes. The kicker was when he suggested recording us being intimate. I was nervous because I'd never seen myself have sex before.

I thought I would look awkward and foolish, but that wasn't the case. As we watched it back, I actually looked good throwing my ass in a circle and got aroused seeing how much Gray enjoyed pleasing me. He was attentive and made sure I came multiple times. More than anything, it was the way in which Gray was so affectionate that confirmed I made the right choice in giving us a chance.

In this short amount of time I realized his love language was touch. I was used to laying my head on his chest when we were just friends, but this was different. This man couldn't keep his hands off me. Massages, foot rubs, and forehead kisses were just the tip of the iceberg. When he would walk up behind me and kiss my neck, it made me feel so sexy.

The way Gray intertwined his legs in mine and held me close as we slept made me feel protected and safe. In the streets, he was this ruthless bill collector who showed no mercy and would end your life without feeling any remorse. But with me, Gray was this loveable, caring, handsome man whose only goal was to see me happy.

When I finally pulled up to my place, Harmony was already there. She exited her car when she saw me parking.

"Hey, boo. Were you waitin' long?" I quizzed when I got out of my car.

"Umm, yes! What the hell took you so long?" I smiled then pursed my lips.

"Y'all nasty. He held you hostage for three damn days. Wasn't that enough?" Harmony laughed.

"I sorta initiated it. Girl, I can't get enough of that man. I'm obsessed with him already. They said good things come to those that wait, and they neva lied. Gray is the best thing that eva happened to me," I admitted.

"Well, damn, it's only been a few days, and you came to that conclusion already? The dick must be dickin'. Is that nigga holdin' a bat between his legs?" Harmony raised her brows.

"It's perfect, not too big or too small, just the right length and girth. Which I'm happy 'bout 'cause I can't handle a big ass dick. I'm already breathin' deep and bracin' for impact. Gray knows exactly what he's doin'. All these years wit' Jamal's dirty ass and this was the first time I experienced back to back orgasms. I'm talkin' three to four every single time. I feel cheated and robbed." I shook my head.

"Well, I'm happy for you and glad y'all finally got together. Now, do I get my friend back?" She smiled.

"Yes, you know how it is when you first get wit' someone. But I promise to make time for you, always." I hugged Harmony. "Let's go inside."

When I unlocked the door and pushed it open, I was floored. Someone had broken in and destroyed my place. My furniture was sliced open, the words slut and whore were written all over the walls in spray paint, and my flat screen tv was cracked, like someone hit it with a bat.

"Oh my fuckin' God. I don't believe this shit." I immediately started crying. "This has Jamal written all over it."

Harmony walked into the kitchen.

"Jesus... I don't think this was Jamal."

"Why?" I questioned, entering the kitchen.

All the contents of my cabinets were on the floor, including everything from the fridge and freezer. There was a message left for me on the wall written with lipstick, warning me to stay away from her man. I have no idea who "her" was.

"This is some sick shit. Does she mean Jamal or Gray?" Harmony inquired.

"No one knows 'bout me and Gray, so she must mean Jamal." I pulled out my phone to call him. He answered right away. "One of yo bitches broke into my house and destroyed it. I don't even know how they got in 'cause the locks were changed, but you had to tell the whore my address." He asked me to put him on Facetime, so he could see it for himself.

"I had nothin' to do wit' that and would neva give someone yo address. I know I fucked up puttin' my hands on you, but I'm not an animal, Rain."

Harmony went into the bedroom and came back out.

"The bedroom window is broken. She must have gotten in that way."

"Oh, that bitch is there. Harmony, my sistas are gonna bust yo ass for pullin' that knife out on me, so be ready."

"Fuck you and yo ugly ass sistas. Thanks for the warnin', though. But they need to worry 'bout animal control pickin' 'em up, instead of tryin' to fight yo battles. They're a long way home from their natural habitat. You can't tell me those bitches aren't two hammer-headed bats," Harmony fired back.

"Like I said, they comin' for you. And Rain, I don't know who did that shit, but I'll pay for the damages. Can we meet up and talk? Babe, I wanna make shit right between us and—"

"She ain't yo babe and has moved on. You need to do the same, fuck boy," Harmony yelled.

"Moved on? Wit' who? How—"

Harmony snatched my phone and ended the call.

"I saw the look on yo face when he said can y'all meet up. Don't let him play on yo top. He's a manipulator."

"Hearin' him call me babe was why my face looked like that. The expression was shock, not forgiveness. For him to think we can just pick right back up where we left off is crazy. I have no plans on goin' backwards. Jamal and I are finished. Gray is the only man for me," I affirmed.

"Well, you can't get shit outta here. All yo clothes are piled up and covered in red paint. Whoever this ho is lost her damn mind. I'mma whip her ass when we find out who she is," Harmony threatened.

"Not if I get my hands on her first."

"You neva had a fight in yo life. And from the look of yo apartment, this bitch is unhinged. I don't think you can win, friend." Harmony smirked.

"Just 'cause I don't fight doesn't mean I can't fight. I pulled that cashier off of you didn't I?" I matched her energy, since she wanted to be funny.

"See, that's the difference between you and me. If that was you fightin', I woulda jumped in when you threw the first punch."

"But it was a fair fight. So, umm, yeah." I cut my eyes.

"Where I come from, there is no fair fights. I've been jumped so many times I lost count. Even though we only lived blocks away, growing up in the projects versus a street like this where everyone gets along is completely different. If we didn't go to the same schools, you and I woulda neva met and became friends. We from two different worlds, but I'm glad

77

we did 'cause yo house was an escape for me. You have no idea."

Even though Harmony and I have been friends most of our lives, I only been inside her house once. We spent most of the time at my house, and she stayed every weekend with us, even some holidays. I loved it, being that I was an only child. She had older siblings, but they didn't get along. Most of her fights were with them.

Once we entered high school and started being distracted by boys, we spent less time together but still remained the best of friends.

"I'm ready to go. I will call the leasin' office and let 'em know I'm movin' out. There's no way I can stay here. It's too damn much. Gray is gonna lose his shit when I tell him this." I blew my breath.

* * *

"Hey, Harmony. It's so good to see you."

"Same to you, Momma Deb." They hugged each other.

Harmony always looked at my mom as a second mother. The bond they shared was special.

"Mom, you not gone believe this."

"What happened now?"

She twisted up her face and ushered us into the kitchen. I explained to her how my apartment looked, and the conversation I had with Jamal.

"He's a liar. Jamal knows exactly who did it. What's the

odds that you change the locks and end the relationship, and all of a sudden someone breaks in." My dad entered the room.

"Things seem to be escalating, and I don't like what I'm hearing. If Gray doesn't handle him, I will. Enough is enough," he spewed.

"Honey, there's no need for you to get involved. I'm sure Gray is handling it."

"Y'all heard what I said." My dad exited the kitchen after responding to my mom.

It was rare to see him pissed and short-tempered, especially toward me. There were rumors in the streets that Mr. Ellington had another side to him. People said he was involved with the mob and that his construction business wasn't on the up and up. I questioned Gray about it before, and he didn't deny or confirm the allegations, just smiled. That was enough for me to know they were true and to mind my business.

The way my mom closed her eyes and shook her head when my dad walked away let me know she knew exactly who her husband was and the reach he had. Now, I understood why Deborah Ellington pushed for me to be with a man like Gray. Him and my dad were cut from the same cloth.

"Oh, let me get the package that came for you. I don't know who it's from because it doesn't have a return address. The mailman must have dropped it off. It was in the mailbox."

My mom got up and came back with a small, rectangular box. When I opened it up and saw what was inside, I couldn't believe my eyes.

"What type of sick shit is this?" I started to shake.

"Let me see." Harmony snatched the box.

"Oh, hell no. Y'all might have to call the police."

My mom took the box and pulled the contents out. Inside was an obituary, like the one they passed out at funerals with my picture on it. The pic was from a newspaper clipping when I volunteered at a youth center while in high school and received an award at a banquet they had. Anyone could have gained access to that photo from Google, cropped it, and had it put on there.

When she opened it up, the inside was blank but a dried up flower fell out of it. It was a black rose. A symbol of death and destruction. For the first time ever, I was scared for my life.

Chapter Nine

GRAY

"Are y'all sure this is the right house?" I quizzed. "We can't be runnin' up in the wrong shit."

Bear, Ant, and I were posted outside a house Jamal was supposedly staying at. The day I excused myself to make some calls when I was at the Ellingtons, I reached out to Bear and Ant. They were informed of the situation at hand and were told to offer five grand to anyone who gave up Jamal's location.

Of course his broke, black ass was shacked up with another woman, using her like he used Rain. I wanted to put my hands on this nigga a long time ago, but I knew if I did, Rain would of been forced to choose her man over me. Having her in my life was more important than my ego, so I played my position.

It wasn't easy sitting in the background watching her love

another man, but I did it. Now that he fucked up royally with her, his ass was mine. I promised Rain I wouldn't kill him, so anything other than that was within reason.

"Absolutely. The chick that gave him up had video proof. She said he was fuckin' wit' her sista, but they didn't get along anymore 'cause of him." Bear confirmed. "This is her sista's house, so I know for a fact he in there."

"How the fuck y'all find that info out so fast?" I questioned.

"Shit, I told Kira to put the word out. You know she be in everybody's business. I had to agree to get her hair and nails done, though. And the first thing her stankin' ass did was post a video wit' the money I gave her, talkin' 'bout her man always spoilin' her in the caption." Ant shook his head.

"Just wave the white flag 'cause her crazy ass ain't neva leavin'. And I think you like the wild shit she be doin' and still fuckin' her, so I'm definitely stayin' out y'all shit for now on. My only concern is my niece. Fuck both of you toxic muthafuckas." Bear laughed.

"Man, as soon as she agreed to let me hit and her bra and panties didn't match when she stripped, my ass shoulda got up outta there. That's a clear sign they gone be crazy as hell wit' good pussy that keeps you comin' back. And if the underwire is pokin' through the fabric of the bra, and her panties got a couple holes in it, you definitely gonna need a restrainin' order. They don't give a fuck 'bout shit," Ant informed us. "And speaking of good pussy and fuckin', how's Rain? You went MIA on our asses."

"Bruh, it was definitely worth the wait. That's my wife. I just didn't propose yet."

"So, what about Zia?" Bear inquired. "You just gonna go ghost on her ass."

"I messaged her that we were done with our lil situation when I was in the car with Rain, on the way to my house. She texted back 'oh, really'. It wasn't like we were a couple, so I don't give a fuck. I was very upfront from the beginnin' 'bout what I wanted from her, and she agreed to it. We neva even kissed 'cause it's too intimate," I explained.

"You may not have caught feelings, but she definitely did. When they say 'oh, really', it's the calm before the storm. Be careful. She comin' for yo ass. You been fuckin' her for years. Then you just abruptly end it in a text message. You didn't even have the decency to tell her to her face." Ant laughed. "Welcome to my world. You 'bout to have a Kira on yo hands. I think you should apologize."

"I don't owe some chick I was lettin' suck my dick no explanation or an apology. She should be thankin' me for all the top tier orgasms I provided her wit' over the years. We both got what we needed out of it. I have no regrets." I shrugged my shoulders.

"It's okay to admit you liked her a lil bit. How could you not?" Ant laughed. "Therefore, you need to just say sorry for not tellin' her in person."

I couldn't believe the one with the most drama in their life was telling me what was wrong and right.

"I'll do it, only if you agree to shut the fuck up." I pulled out my phone and sent Zia a message.

When my phone binged, Ant grabbed it.

"Yeah, sleep wit' one eye open, nigga."

Ant handed me the phone back. Zia sent the middle finger emoji.

"Man, I don't give a damn 'bout that. She'll be a'ight," I responded. "Let's go snatch this nigga and be out."

We exited the unmarked van we used for situations like this dressed in all black with our faces covered. The van had fake plates and couldn't be traced back to anyone. Bear kicked in the front door, and we followed him inside. Jamal came running out of the bedroom to see what was going on, and Ant busted that muthafucka in his shit as soon as he turned the corner.

He dropped to the floor, and I placed a bag over his head then stomped him in the stomach after zip tying his hands behind his back.

"What the hell is goin' on?" The chick he was fucking with came rushing into the living room. "Oh, hell. I see y'all got things under control. I'mma go mind my business."

She spun on her heels and went back into the bedroom and closed the door. We dragged Jamal outside and tossed his ass into the back of the van. Ant and I hopped inside with him while Bear ran around to the driver side. Once he pulled out and turned the corner, we took our face coverings off.

"Yo, who the fuck are you niggas? I ain't even do shit to nobody," Jamal whined.

"You like to put yo hands on women, so I would beg to differ," I scoffed.

"Nah, y'all got the wrong guy."

"Nigga, shut the fuck up." Ant kicked him in the head.

Bear drove to the warehouse we used for storage. Our vehicles were already parked out front. As soon as Rain left, I was out the door a few minutes later to meet up with the guys here.

When the doors to the back of the van opened up, I kicked Jamal out of it. We dragged him by his feet inside. He was crying and pleading for his life. I snatched the bag from off his head and kneeled down next to him.

"Ah, shit, come on, Gray. You know I would neva hurt Rain. She tried to keep me from enterin' the house, and I just pushed her a lil. If she said anythin' else, it's not true."

"So, you callin' my girl a liar?" I quizzed.

"Yo girl?" Jamal looked surprised. "Wow, Harmony said she moved on, but I thought she said that to get under my skin. Ain't this a bitch. I always knew that fake ass best friend shit y'all claimed was a lie from the jump."

"Nah, it wasn't. She actually loved yo sorry ass. Rain defended you against everyone, includin' me. You fucked up, so now she is mine, and I don't appreciate how you treated her. And puttin' yo hands on her was a dummy move, knowin' how I get down. You from the streets, nigga. Don't act like you don't know."

I stood up and kicked Jamal in his mouth, busting his shit wide open. Before I could continue my assault, my phone rang. It was Rain. I connected the call.

85

"Yo, stop cryin'. I can't understand you. Take a deep breath and say it again." Anger filled my body as I bit down on my lip and listened to Rain explain what the hell transpired from the time she left my house until now. "Where you at?"

I ended the call and blew my breath.

"What's good? Who was that?" Bear questioned.

"I gotta go check on Rain. Make sure this bitch right here understands where the fuck he went wrong. I'll be back as soon as I can."

Saying I did the dash all the way to Rain's parents' house would be an understatement. I didn't even bother to knock on the door when I got there. It was unlocked, and they were expecting me anyway.

When Rain's eyes met mine, she rushed over and practically jumped in my arms. I kissed the top of her head and rubbed her back.

"I got you," I whispered.

"I'm so glad you're here. This is crazy, and my husband isn't happy right now and wants to intervene. You of all people know what that means." Miss Deb stared at me.

Mr. Ellington was definitely a boss, and those who knew the real him understood his reach and the connections he had. I was one of them.

"He can stand down. I will handle this personally," I informed her.

"It has to be someone Jamal was dealin' wit'." Rain wiped the tears off her face.

"Believe me, I will find out who. Until I do, I want you to

stay at my place. Call yo job and put in an emergency family leave. Yo ass is not comin' back outside 'til the person responsible for all of this is buried beneath my feet."

"You gonna leave me alone in that house?" Rain quizzed.

"There will be a security detail watching the house twenty-four seven. So, when I gotta run out and handle business, you good. And Harmony hood ass can stay and provide security on the inside." We laughed.

"I got a car payment and rent to pay. A bitch gotta go to work." Harmony frowned her face at me.

"I'll pay you $1,000 a day."

"Rain, grab yo shit and let's go home. I'll even cook and clean."

"Gray, can I talk to you for a minute alone?" Miss Deb asked.

She walked out of the kitchen, and I followed her into the office they had in the back of the house. When Miss Deb closed the door behind us, I knew whatever she wanted to say was serious.

"There's something you need to know about Rain. I was going to allow her to tell you on her own time, but since time is of the essence, you need to know now. She suffers from DID, which stands for dissociative identity disorder. The other personality Rain has is named Storm, and that's exactly what it feels like when she shows up."

I looked at Miss Deb like she had lost her damn mind.

"If Rain suffered from mental illness, I would know. This isn't makin' any sense."

"That's because she does a great job at keeping Storm suppressed, but stressful situations can lead Rain into a state of depression," Miss Deb explained.

"Since when?" I quizzed. "I've been 'round you guys my whole life."

"After the fire that killed my parents. Rain blamed herself and spiraled out of control. She fell into a deep depression. Out of nowhere, she started acting strange and talking crazy. And you know Rain is sweet and kind, but she became angry and mean toward everyone. Then one day she woke up, cut all her hair off, and said her name was Storm. We had to have her committed to a psychiatric unit for adolescents." Miss Deb's eyes filled with tears. "I didn't even recognize my own child anymore."

"I remember when Rain went away, but you guys said she was visiting Mr. Ellington's parents."

"We didn't know what we were dealing with and wanted it to stay a private matter. When Rain becomes Storm, then goes back to Rain, she doesn't remember anything Storm does or says. They are completely two different people with two distinct personalities. They said the trauma of the fire caused all of this. It was Rain's way of coping and escaping from the reality of the situation. So, this right here, especially receiving that awful obituary, can cause Rain to get sad and start thinking of the past. To avoid those memories, she will flip on us." I ran my hands down my face.

"How do we stop it from happenin'? Is she on medication?"

"No, and this is why I'm sharing this information with you. The only way to help Rain is to make sure she doesn't become depressed. You are the perfect distraction. She loves and trusts you. Keep her focused on the present. If she starts talking about the past, stop her. Make sure she laughs and stays busy, so she doesn't have time to focus on the negativity surrounding her."

"Yo, this is crazy, no pun intended," I clarified.

"Tell me about it. Harmony will be a huge help to you, so I'm glad she will be with Rain. She is aware of Storm and so is Jamal. They are the only two people who know, outside of my husband and I. Rain has a therapist she sees once a month. This woman is amazing and taught all of us how to help Rain cope. If you think she is going down the rabbit hole, contact her. I'll write down her information and give you my number as well. Whoever is doing this needs to be stopped immediately. We can't afford for Storm to get out. "

After Miss Deb gave me the sheet of paper she wrote the info down on, I tucked it in my pants pocket.

"I'mma put an end to this, I promise. And don't worry 'bout Rain. She's safe wit' me."

"This I know. What I don't know is why you're dressed like you just robbed a bank, but that's none of my business. If you need me I'm here. I'll go next door and let your grandparents know what is going on, and they can come over and have Sunday dinner with us. You just concentrate on keeping my sweet girl safe." Miss Deb smiled.

When we left the office to go back to Rain and Harmony in

the kitchen, Mr. Ellington was descending the steps and gave me a head nod. I excused myself to go speak to him.

"Wassup, Boss Man," I greeted him.

"Do you need my assistance to handle this situation with my daughter? Whoever this person is must not be aware of the lengths we both would go to protect Rain. I know you're willing to go to the depths of hell, and I will go even lower. If their entire living bloodline needs to be taken out while they watch, so be it."

"Me and my guys are on it. We currently have Jamal at the warehouse. I'm headin' back ova there once I leave here," I informed him.

"I went through the surveillance cameras after being made aware of the package being left in our mailbox. The person was dressed in all black and knew not to look up. It was placed there in the middle of the night. I'm removing the mailbox from the end of the walkway and placing it up by the front door. The motion sensors weren't placed out that far because the alarms would go off whenever someone walked by at night." He kissed his teeth.

We talked a few more minutes before Mr. Ellington went back upstairs, and I went into the kitchen.

"Rain, yo car can stay here, and you'll ride wit' me. Harmony will follow us to the house and park in the garage. A security team is already on the way there. I won't leave 'til they are in place."

"I will Facetime time you. And now I can sleep at night

knowin' you are safe. I love you, sweet girl." Miss Deb hugged Rain then Harmony before we left.

Everything Ant said was playing back in my mind as I drove to my beach house. Rain was convinced this was someone Jamal was dealing with, but I wasn't. All this happened the minute we got together. The only person who would have a problem with that was Zia.

She knew about the friendship Rain and I shared. I even told her Rain was the reason we could never be more than what we were. Even though we had a mutual agreement, she was still a woman. Judging by her response to me, Zia was definitely in her feelings. Therefore, it was time to pay her an unfriendly visit.

Chapter Ten

JAMAL JOHNSON

"Ugghhh, fuck." These niggas were working me over good.

"Listen, we can do this shit all day and night. All you have to do is tell us who the bitch is that's fuckin' wit' Rain, and we'll stop," Bear uttered before crushing my fingers beneath his feet again.

They untied me after Gray left and had me lay on my stomach, face down, with my hands out. He acted as if he was stepping on a fucking bug, the way he pressed and twisted his sneakers into my hands. All I had on was some boxer shorts and socks.

"I can't tell you somethin' I don't know. This is the first time I'm hearin' 'bout someone fuckin' wit her. Let me go, and I'll see what I can find out," I pleaded.

"Keep playin' stupid and yo fingers gone look like potted meat by the time we get done," Ant spewed.

I don't know where the hell he got a meat mallet from, but this muthafucka started pounding on my fingers like they were strips of chicken. Bear stepped on my wrists to prevent me from moving my hands. The pain was excruciating. I could see the ligaments, tendons, and bones.

"So, you had no idea her apartment was trashed? And right after she threw yo sorry ass out. I find that very hard to believe," Bear stated.

"Honestly, this is all news to me. I wasn't the best boyfriend to Rain, but I didn't have nothin' to do wit' this shit. Y'all questionin' the wrong person."

After Rain put me out, I never went back to the apartment. There was no reason for me to ever step foot in there again. They had destroyed everything I owned and put it out for trash.

"Well, who the fuck should we be askin'?" Ant quizzed.

"Rain's triflin' ass best friend. I bet my life Harmony ass is behind this. Rain changed the locks, so there was no way I could get in," I explained. "And Harmony helped her destroy my shit, and it was probably her idea to begin wit'. The way they did my Jordans and put my clothes in black trash bags was some hood shit. Rain isn't like that, but we all know Harmony is."

"Hold the fuck up. Why would Harmony do this?" Bear questioned.

"Jealousy. Harmony wants to be Rain. This shit is deeper than y'all think." I shook my head.

"Sit cho bitch ass up." Ant kicked me in my side.

"Ahhhhh!" It felt like my ribs cracked. I pushed up on my elbows in order to sit on my knees. My fingers were broken and useless. "I can't tell you what I know if you puncture my lungs."

"Let his punk ass talk. If the shit doesn't sound like it's addin' up, we'll kick his teeth down his throat." Bear was the meanest of the two.

We all grew up together, so I could tell them apart by their mannerisms. Ant always had a silly ass grin on his face while Bear was more serious. Just as I was about to explain my side, Gray walked back into the warehouse they had me in.

"Is this muthafucka talkin' yet?" he quizzed.

"Yeah, but you ain't gone like what the fuck he sayin'. The shit is wild and hard to believe." Ant grinned.

"Well, at this point he's our only lead. I just left Zia's house. After holding her and the dog at gunpoint, I realized she couldn't have done it. Her ass hasn't left the house since receiving my message. She smelled like she needed a bath. There were candy wrappers in her bed and empty fast food containers and pizza boxes on the floor. Zia is over there going through the motions. Ant was right for once in his life. She definitely caught feelings." Gray blew his breath. "So, what is this nigga sayin'?"

"I'm sayin' Harmony is the one y'all need to snatch up and beat down. If you and Rain are together forreal, she's the one you want, not me."

"Nah, I don't believe that shit." Gray ran his hands down

his face. "Why? What the fuck does she gain from doin' this? That's her best friend. They're more like sisters than friends actually."

"Harmony is jealous of Rain. She wants her life and to be her. I tried to tell Rain, but she wouldn't listen. Whenever I brought it up, Rain said I was the one who was jealous and needed to worry 'bout myself. I saw the way Harmony looked at Rain sometimes, and I didn't like it. Yes, I know I'm the last one who should comment on how someone treated Rain, but it even creeped me out. I know the real Harmony, so one day I broke into her car to get my hands on this sketchbook she's always drawing in but won't let no one see. Her old car didn't have an alarm on it. All the pictures were of you and her."

"Me and Rain?" Gray quizzed.

"Nah, you and Harmony. She made it look like y'all was a couple. There was one drawing of Rain, but she was layin' on a bed of black roses. That's some sick shit. I neva told Rain what I saw 'cause she wouldn't believe me no way. Harmony is obsessed wit' you. So, whateva you think I did, it was her."

I could tell by Gray's expression he believed what I said. When I mentioned the black roses, he furrowed his brow.

"Where does she keep the sketchbook? You not a man of yo word, so everythin' you sayin' needs to be fact checked." Gray squatted down next to me. "And if yo ass is lyin', I'mma personally watch Bear and Ant cut you into pieces, place you inside a garbage bag, and sit it on yo mom's steps on a Sunday mornin'. You'll be the first thing she sees on her way to church. She still goes to Second Baptist, right?" I nodded my head. "I'd do it myself, but I promised Rain I wouldn't kill you."

The way Gray defended and protected Rain made me laugh inside. You would think him and Rain were fucking. I would never go as hard as he did for her, and we were together for ten years. This nigga really kidnapped me from my new chick's house, like some gangsta shit you see in the movies.

Everyone knew the legacy of his family, so when Gray became the bill collector people understood he would be just as ruthless as his dad. They were both trained by the best. My dad used to tell me stories about the Deeds. He also said Mr. Ellington wasn't to be played with and to stay away from the both of them.

The only reason I even got with Rain was because Harmony told me she was a virgin. Now that I think about it, she was never her friend and only wanted me around to keep Rain and Gray from becoming a couple. Harmony bet me twenty dollars that Rain wouldn't give it up to me. Once Rain gave into my pursuit of her, my only goal was to get the pussy and bounce.

Months went by before she even let me touch it. She still wasn't trying to let me hit and planned on saving herself for marriage, then the fire happened. That changed the course of our entire relationship. Rain went through so much during her depression and personality changes, and I stood right by her, hoping the entire situation made her vulnerable. And it did.

Rain couldn't believe I stayed after seeing her as Storm.

When she got out of the hospital I visited her every day and never told anyone her secret. I had invested too much of my time to walk away empty handed. She fell for me hard and gave it up one night when her parents went to dinner and left us alone in the house. They were thankful to me as well and trusted their daughter with me.

She was green about everything, so I had her watch a couple pornos in order for her to get the idea of what to do. I walked Rain through the rest. It wasn't the first time I took someones' virginity, so I made Rain suck me off first. That virgin pussy made me cum too fast. Getting the first one out of the way always helped with that.

Once I got what I set out to get, I wanted to end it with Rain. She was definitely worth the wait, but I wasn't the type to be with just one woman. I wanted to taste the rainbow and dip my stick in every pot of gold waiting at the end of it, but Harmony threatened to tell her about the bet. I knew her father would probably kill me if he found out, so that was when I decided to be the worst man ever to Rain, hoping she would leave me instead.

When her father offered me a position in his company, I was pissed. They wanted her to leave me alone as well, but whatever Rain wanted she got. Her parents' only goal in life was to make Rain happy. I knew making Mr. Ellington lose money and fucking with his reputation would put an end to that fast. He would have no choice but to discipline me, which would cause problems with Rain and I.

The only thing I couldn't figure out was why Harmony all of a sudden was on board with Rain breaking up with me. Seeing her at the house enraged me, which was why I pushed both of them out of my way. She had me by the balls all these years then just released them without explanation. Harmony had an end game. I just didn't know what it was.

"She got a new car but kept it in the trunk of the old one where the spare tire was. Harmony's crazy ass probably burned it by now."

"Bear, contact the security team and tell 'em to steal Harmony keys without her knowin' and check her car from the inside out. I want pics of anythin' that looks like it doesn't belong. I'mma Facetime Rain and act like I'm just checkin' in on them. I need to make sure Harmony is within my eyesight."

Gray stepped away to make the call. When he did, Ant kicked me in my chest, knocking me over.

"What the fuck was that for?" I tried to sit back up again without using my hands.

"For playin' in Rain's face. She's like a lil sista to me, muthafucka. You take somethin' so sacred from her ova a fuckin' bet was foul as hell. The shit you and Harmony did was heartless as hell. Where the fuck I put my meat mallet."

When Ant said that, I tried to get away by rolling on the ground. I didn't get too far before he caught up to me, snatched the back of my neck, and started beating me in the face with the mallet. I started leaking from everywhere, eyes, nose, and mouth.

"Yo, chill." Bear laughed. "You got his face lookin' like it went through a meat grinder."

My right eye started closing up, and there was ringing in my ears. It felt like my entire face instantly swelled up and started burning. I knew at that very moment I was in my final resting place. Gray may have promised Rain he wouldn't kill me, but that didn't stop him from giving the okay for Ant and Bear to do it.

There was no way in hell he would let me walk out of here after learning what I did to the only woman he ever loved. He sat on the sidelines and waited patiently for Rain. If that wasn't love, then I don't know what love was.

"Can y'all at least make sure my mom gets some type of notice that I'm gone or put my body where she can find it?" I could barely speak.

"Muthafucka, we not Hallmark. You shoulda been a better son, and yo ass wouldn't be here," Ant spewed.

Gray reappeared, and Bear showed him his phone. I don't know what they were looking at, but all three of them focused their eyes on me.

"They didn't find the sketches, but something else was found that solidified yo story. With that bein' said, I'm sure you know things aren't gonna end well for you or Harmony. Her fate will be a lil different than yours, though. She deserves to suffer for a long time. I think you suffered enough."

As soon as Gray stopped talking, Bear and Ant each grabbed one of my arms. They dragged me over to the other side of the warehouse to a pine casket. After placing me inside, they mixed something together in a large container. I realized it was concrete once they started pouring it over me. Being shot in the head would have been better. Right before they covered my face, I heard Gray say he texted the cleanup crew already. Who knew his voice would be the last one I heard before leaving this earth.

Chapter Eleven

RAIN

"Hey, handsome." I greeted Gray when he walked into the kitchen and over to the bar where Harmony and I were sitting. "You good?"

"Yeah, now that I see you." He smiled and bent over to give me a kiss.

"This is a beautiful place you have here, Gray. I might need to holla at Ant, if y'all doin' it like this. Kira's crazy ass already got one foot out the door. I'm sure I can help her get the other one out. Fuckin' wit' people is my specialty," Harmony boasted.

"Is that right?" Gray grinned at her.

It wasn't a good grin either, but you would have to know Gray intimately to realize he only made that expression if he was sizing you up. Why he would do that to Harmony was a mystery to me, and I planned on asking him about it later when we were alone.

"Well, maybe you need to take the lead on findin' the stank, lonely, jealous, miserable, rotten pussy ass bitch who's fuckin' wit' yo best friend. For some reason we keep comin' up empty handed." Gray kissed his teeth.

Harmony bit down on her bottom lip and cut her eyes before answering.

"Believe me, I want the ho just as much as you do, but she must be very experienced at stalking or have help 'cause she's always one step ahead. And I believe it's Jamal. Rain told me you were gonna go after him for puttin' his hands on her but promised not to kill him. That muthafucka needs to go. He'll neva tell you the truth 'cause then he tells on himself." Harmony shrugged her shoulders.

"I already talked to Jamal. That's where I'm comin' from," Gray informed us.

Harmony held her breath and appeared to lose a little color in her face. She almost looked flustered. I'd never seen her like this before. My friend always held it together, and not to mention, she was beautiful.

Her hair stayed slayed, she had flawless, caramel skin, and a cute shape. Even though she dressed down the majority of the time, her slim thick curves were still visible. Besides her rough around the edges attitude, Harmony was a catch but never wanted to settle down with just one guy. She always spoke up for herself and didn't take shit from no one, which I admired.

"What did he say? Did he give you any leads?" she inquired.

"Nah, he admitted all the shit he did to Rain was fucked up but denied any involvement in what's goin' on now. The chick he fuckin' was scary as hell, so there's no way she was bold enough to break into Rain's house and leave a package in the middle of the night in a mailbox. Jamal was basically a dead end."

"How did you know it was the middle of the night?" Harmony questioned Gray.

"Mr. Ellington looked at the cameras, which she seemingly knew were there, so I wouldn't be surprised if it ends up bein' someone we all know. She's probably ate a lot of paint chips when she was lil that fucked up her thought process."

"Did you keep yo promise to me in regards to Jamal?" I stared at him.

"Absolutely, I'm a man of my word." Gray kissed my forehead.

"Since he couldn't help, she's still out there plottin' her next move on me. I don't wanna live like a prisoner. It will drive me insane. I'm already startin' to feel a lil rattled. This shit is depressin'." I sighed.

"Friend, you know we not gone let nothin' happen to you." Harmony gave me a hug.

"How 'bout we take a vacation to an island. Get you outta here for like a month, so you can move around freely and not worry at all. The last thin' I want is for you to be stressed," Gray suggested.

"I would love that. Can we leave tonight?" I laughed.

"In three days. I need time to get everythin' set up. Meanwhile, I'mma get outta these clothes and hop in the shower. You care to join me." Gray licked his lips.

"You forgot we got company. That's rude."

"Shit, Harmony not company, she's family. But right now, her ass is hired help. She can clean up or start a load of laundry while we disappear for a few." Gray ran his hands over his waves.

He was so damn fine, it didn't make any sense. I got up and wrapped my hands around his waist. Gray squeezed my ass with both hands then made it shake while pressing his lips against mine.

"Whateva, you better check the forecast before plannin' that trip and make sure there's not a storm comin'," Harmony shot back.

When those words left her mouth, I swung my head so fast in Harmony's direction it made me dizzy for a second. Her words were laced with so much venom and sarcasm. Gray may not have known what she meant, but I did.

"Excuse me?" I released my arms from around Gray and turned to face Harmony.

"We in the beginnin' of hurricane season. That's all I meant, relax."

I didn't appreciate the smirk on Harmony's face. Something weird was going on with her. Maybe all the shit she had done to people was finally catching up with her, causing my best friend to act other than self.

People posted the fight she had in the dollar store on social media, so that could be it. They were clowning her for needing my help. She said it didn't bother her, but Harmony's actions today said otherwise.

"Let's go." Gray grabbed my hand and led the way to his master bedroom.

"We gone have to be quiet, since Harmony is downstairs. I don't want her to hear us."

This man started taking off my clothes as soon as he closed the door behind us.

"Shit, this is our house. We don't have to be quiet for no damn body," Gray responded.

"Our house?"

"Yo ass heard exactly what the fuck I said, our house. You and me." He pinched my nipple and laughed then took off his sweats. "And if you try to hold back, I'll take you downstairs, bend yo ass over, and give Harmony a front row view of our nastiness," Gray threatened.

"Maybe I need to choose Grayson. He would neva." I laughed.

"Too late, Gray already has his dick out."

I looked down and saw that Gray had indeed dropped his boxers. He finished undressing as I watched. On our way to the shower, Gray walked over to what looked like an intercom on the wall and pushed a button.

"What are you up to?"

"Nothin', I just want to make sure the switch to the intercom was off. My IT guy programmed it to where you could hear anythin' that was said in here throughout the entire house. This way if I see someone on the cameras doin' some fuck shit, I can yell out to 'em."

Gray did have a security system set up in the room, but it was hidden in a chest. You wouldn't even know it was there and could see every part of the house.

After the shower, I didn't even make it to the bed before Gray was on my heels. He snatched the towel from around me and pulled me into his arms. When he placed me up against the wall and lifted my big ass up, allowing my legs to rest in the crooks of his arms, I knew I was in for a good time.

"Mmmmm." I moaned as Gray slid right up in me.

He wasted no time putting in that work. This man pounded away while tucking in his bottom lips and staring into my eyes.

"I'mma make you cum so many times, yo ass might pass out. This is my pussy."

"Sssssssss, it feels so good, babe." I cooed.

"It'll feel even betta when you bust one. The shit already gushy."

Gray sucked on my titties while I pressed my fingers into his back. I kept my nails short, so instead of him being left with scratches, he had fingerprint marks.

"You 'bout to make cum." My voice was high pitched. "Ahhhhh."

He increased his speed and silenced me with a kiss. We let out tongues dance as my pussy throbbed and released its nectar. My legs shook in his arms.

"Damn, this some good shit. It's like a fuckin drug, and I love gettin' high off yo pussy."

Gray nibbled on my ear before putting me down. His dick was still stiff as a board. I didn't even get a chance to take a deep breath before he had me on the carpet with his head buried between my legs, sucking on my clit.

It was still swollen and tingly. The sensation I felt was out of this world. All types of sounds came out of my mouth as he sucked and slurped me into another orgasm. My pussy was soaking wet at this point.

"Turn over."

I did as I was told, and he plunged right back inside my pussy and fucked me good. My legs were spread wide open, and I tossed my ass back at him while looking over my shoulder. He smiled at me and raised his eyebrows, making me even wetter.

"Ugh, goddamn, Gray."

He pressed his hand on the small of my back, and his strokes became short and fast, which was a clear sign Gray was about to cum. I rubbed on my clit as he continued his assault, so we could bust together.

"Fuck!" he yelled, pulling out and releasing his seeds.

I came at the same time the warm fluid splattered on my ass. Gray reached over and grabbed his shirt that was on the floor not too far from us and wiped off the evidence of his enjoyment.

"Whew, that was a much needed stress reliever. You are the perfect distraction." I batted my eyes at Gray.

"That was just a warm up." He helped me up off the floor

then went back to the intercom. Gray was definitely up to something. "I'mma 'bout to run you a tub, then we can order out. The chef is comin' in tonight to make dinner."

Gray ended up taking another shower while I relaxed in a bubble bath. He had a wine cooler in the sitting area of the bedroom and poured me up a glass of champagne.

"When did you plan on telling' me 'about Storm?" he quizzed, catching me off guard as he sat on the edge of the tub. "And don't act dumb. Yo mom already told me everything'."

"Once again, she had no right to tell you my business. I wanted to inform you 'bout Storm on my own time, when I was ready." I shook my head.

"And by the time you did, she coulda showed back up in you, leavin' me confused and concerned. If I woulda went to bed nestled up next to Lizzo and woke up to Mike Tyson standin' over me, I might have punched you in the face." He laughed.

"I was scared you would think I was a freak. Most people who suffer from mental illness are mistreated at some point, and usually by family or the people responsible for taking care of 'em. They make jokes that are not funny, call you names, or say dumb shit 'cause they don't understand what you're goin' through. Being in that facility was the worst experience ever. They helped get me better, but not all the staff was nice. Some were mean and easily aggravated."

I could feel the tears trying to make an entrance.

"I'm sorry you had that experience. I know more 'bout mental illness than you think. My mom suffers from it too. I just don't say much 'cause like you said, most people don't have the patience for it. It wasn't 'til I got older and did my own research that I learned how to handle my mom whenever she showed up. She's bipolar and doesn't take her medication consistently," he confessed.

"Wow, I knew she had issues but not that. I'm sorry."

"It's all good. I used to get mad at her, but now I just enjoy the moments we get to share. Whenever she's ready, I'mma put her in the best facility money can buy. If she's there for at least six months to a year, she should be straight. The medicine needs time to get in her system to see if it's workin'. This way they know how to adjust it. Her ass won't comply long enough. Since she always voluntarily agrees to get screened and admits herself, my mom checks out before she sees the judge. If she's not a harm to herself or others, they have to let her leave. The system is fucked up." Gray sighed.

"Especially if you don't have adequate insurance. My parents pay for the best psychotherapy. Everyone can't afford that. And I apologize for not sharin' Storm wit' you sooner. I have her under control. If I feel like I'm spiralin', I'll let you know. My support system is even stronger now wit' you on board. Havin' people who love me to advocate for my mental well bein' when I can't do it for myself is huge. It can be the difference between sane and insane or life and death in some cases." I down the rest of my bubbly.

"This situation is definitely stressful, but it'll be comin' to an end soon. All I want you to worry 'bout is which island you want to call home for a month."

Now that Gray knew about Storm, another weight had been lifted off my shoulders. Once he figured out who was making my life a living hell over a man I was no longer with, we could move on with our life together.

Wait... none of this started happenin' 'til I got with Gray. Maybe this had absolutely nothin' to do with Jamal and everythin' to do with him.

Chapter Twelve

HARMONY SMITH

I can't believe I'm listenin' to these muthafuckas fuck in surround sound!

About fifteen minutes after Gray and Rain went upstairs, the sounds of them fucking could be heard throughout the house. No matter where I went I heard them, even in the bathroom.

Listening to Rain moan out in pleasure made me sick to my stomach. Gray should have been making love to me, not her. She didn't deserve him. He belonged with a woman who could match his energy, not some fat bitch who had a whole other person living inside their head.

Everyone thought I was so lucky to have Rain as my best friend. For some reason people were drawn to her. Granted, she had a nice personality and would do anything for you. Besides that, there wasn't anything special about Rain Ellington.

The only reason I initially became her friend was because she always had the best snacks, which she shared with me, and money to buy stuff at the events they had at school, like the book fair. Rain would do anything I said too. In a way, I bullied her, along with the other kids. Once she invited me over to her house, and I saw where and how she lived, I made her my best friend.

Staying with the Ellingtons was a break from the crowded ass project apartment I lived in, where I had to share a room with my sisters. It was four of us. The room was too tight to fit multiple beds, so we shared a bunk bed. I slept on the top bunk with one of my sisters who peed on herself until the age of fourteen.

My obsession for Gray started when we were in high school. I became cool with him because of Rain, being that they were neighbors. He had always been cute, but once puberty took over and his ass morphed into a handsome young man, my heart skipped a beat. Whenever I was at her house I tried to get Gray to notice me, but he only had eyes for Rain and made it very clear to everyone.

Honestly, I was offended that he wanted her over me. In my eyes, I was the cat's meow while she was just okay. Rain was pretty. There was no denying that, but she didn't hold a candle next to me, but for some reason all the niggas wanted her. It was like she released pheromones wherever she went that made her desirable. I hated it.

All the guys I dealt with always had someone else. No one wanted to make me their number one. I always came in second and third, sometimes even fourth. Meanwhile, this ho had the most desirable man in our school, but was worried about their raggedy ass friendship. She was also a virgin and planned on saving herself for marriage. Well, I was determined that person wouldn't be Gray Deeds, so I made a bet with Jamal's slow ass.

I only wanted him to be with Rain in order to keep her away from Gray because he was wearing her down. There were a few times she thought about giving him a shot, but I reminded her of how it would damage their friendship. I convinced her to go with Jamal instead because he was a safe bet, unlike Gray, who came from a family of thugs and would eventually become one. Of course she listened to me. As her best friend, she thought I would never steer her wrong.

Rain was so fucking weak and gullible at times, she made me want to punch her in the face. She got caught up in the web I spun and really hit it off with Jamal's cornball ass. And he played her ass too. It didn't take much to fool her. Rain was so trusting and always wanted to see the good in people, like now. How could she not see me coming? I was hiding right in plain sight. That was the beauty of all this. While she thought the enemy was lurking outside, I was sitting right next to her, smiling.

"I'm 'bout to make us a drink. Do you want one?" Gray asked as he and Rain made their way downstairs.

I was sitting in the living room, lost in my own thoughts.

"Yes, I need one after listenin' to y'all. Animals in the wild don't carry on like that."

"What are you talkin' 'bout?" Rain acted confused.

"I heard y'all fuckin' and didn't appreciate it. It could be heard throughout the entire house." I frowned, disgusted.

"Gray! You said you were makin' sure it was turned off." Rain playfully pushed him.

Seeing them so happy and carefree made me want to vomit.

"My bad. I must have turned it on by accident. I hope we didn't disturb you."

Gray smirked. His smug attitude made me think he did it on purpose. He had been acting funny toward me since he came in.

"I'll take a double shot of Henny on the rocks with a splash of ginger ale."

I got up and followed them into the kitchen.

"Damn, you drink like a grown ass man." I stuck my middle finger up at Gray.

He was getting on my last damn nerve. I was already pissed that he put us on lockdown, fucking up my plans. It was just a minor setback, though. All I had to do was get inside Rain's head when we were alone. Since he decided to take her away, I needed to do something drastic in order to make Storm appear before then. There was no way I could let them leave.

The ace in the hole was that Gray didn't know about Storm. Rain's biggest fear was him finding out. Once he saw her crazy, bald-headed ass in action, Gray would definitely second guess his decision to be with Rain. She would have to go back into the hospital, and then I could make my move on him. When a man was in his feelings, he could easily be comforted and persuaded into doing the wrong thing.

Gray sat my drink down on the bar in front of me. He made him and Rain a Long Island iced tea. That shit had multiple liquors in it, but he wanted to talk about my drink. Something was definitely up with him.

He ended up ordering pizza and putting on a movie. I felt like the third wheel for the first time in my life. Watching them sit all close to each other, sharing the same blanket, enraged me. Gray would massage her scalp or kiss on her neck, making her smile. The relationship she had with Jamal was nothing like this. He would barely hold her hand, let alone display affection for her in front of others.

When Gray slid his hands under the blanket and Rain started giggling, I knew it was time for me to make my exit. After excusing myself, I went to the room I would be staying in and thought about how to ruin the one person who actually cared about me. It was fucked up, but I deserved a happily ever after too.

I ended up falling asleep. Rest wasn't something that came easy to me this last week. My mind was always racing. I sighed as my feet hit the floor. We came right here from Rain's parents' house, so I didn't get a chance to get any of my belongings. If it wasn't for the emergency bag of clothes and shit I kept in my car, I wouldn't have anything right now.

Gray said someone could go to my house to get me some stuff, but I didn't want them going through my things. He said it was best if Rain and I stayed put until all of this was over with.

I hopped in the shower to freshen up and changed my clothes. On my way downstairs, I could hear people talking. *Damn, how long did I sleep?* I looked at my phone and realized four hours had passed by.

"Well, look who's finally awake?" Rain laughed as I made my way down the hallway. "I checked on you, but yo ass was knocked out."

"Yeah, I must have really been tired." I cracked a fake smile. "What's goin' on down here?"

"Gray invited everyone over for dinner. I'm just as surprised as you. All he said was that the chef was cookin' dinner tonight. Ant and Bear are the only ones here right now, but more are on the way."

When I peeked my head inside the dining room area, the table was set to feed ten damn people.

"It's a nice surprise, I guess." I shrugged my shoulders.

"I think he wants to tell everyone 'bout us goin' away. Hopefully, he plans on invitin' 'em. A month without seein' any of y'all would be crazy. You definitely have to come. I'm not leavin' without you."

Before I could respond, Gray interrupted us.

"Good, our guest of honor is here." Rain and I both looked at him.

"What are you talkin' 'bout, babe?" she quizzed.

"I know he's not talkin' 'bout my ass." Gray grinned, pissing me off.

"My bad... I thought yo ass would appreciate bein' celebrated for all yo hard work, especially by me. It was my attention you were tryin' to get, right?"

"Stop playin' in my face, Gray." I nervously chewed on the inside of my cheek.

"Someone needs to fill me in on what's goin' on." Rain looked me up and down.

The doorbell rang, putting a pause to our conversation.

"Relax, it will all make sense soon. I just need to let the rest of our guests in. You two stay right here." Gray walked off, leaving me with Rain, who wasn't going to stop being annoying.

"Is somethin' goin' on between y'all that I don't know about? He's been a lil short wit' you, and now he throws a dinner in yo honor. I don't like it."

"Me either. It's weird as fuck, and I'm leavin'." I went to walk away, but was stopped by the sound of Ant's voice.

"You ain't goin' no fuckin' where," he spewed, sipping on a drink.

It seemed like Ant fell from the ceiling. I had no idea he was even standing behind me.

"I don't know who you think you talkin' too, but Kira's funny lookin' ass isn't here," I shot back.

"No, but I can send for her, and she'll beat the shit outta you. Y'all both sip from the same cup of crazy, but I guarantee you her ass crazier. Bear rolled her down my driveway in a recyclin' bin, and she was unphased by it. Got up and walked back in the house, like her ass just got off a ride at Great Adventures." He laughed, like the shit was funny.

"I'll beat fire outta her lopsided ass. You got me all the way fucked up." I put my finger in Ant's face.

"Shit, yo ass couldn't even beat the lady in the dollar store. And if you don't get that raggedy ass finger outta my face, I'll break that bitch."

"Y'all need to stop, and Ant, you wrong for threatenin' a woman." Rain got in between us.

"Rain, the only woman here is you. Harmony's a fuckin' snake." She looked over at me.

"Whoa... Are y'all startin' the festivities without me," Gray quizzed.

He was smiling and rubbing his hands together.

"Babe, what's goin' on? Why would Ant call Harmony a snake? What is this dinner really about?"

"I'll explain everythin' as soon as we sit down."

Gray had us all go into the dining room. I tried to walk in the other direction, but Ant was on my ass. He made me sit at the head of the table. Once everyone was seated, which now included Rain's parents and Gray's grandparents, I knew they must have figured out I was behind the package and destroying Rain's apartment.

I picked up the glass of water that was sitting next to my

place setting and gulped it down. My throat was dry as hell, and I could feel a knot in my stomach forming.

Whateva you do, don't fold. Fuck all these muthafuckas.

"Harmony, do you wanna tell Rain why we're here? I'm sure you figured it out by now, especially after the lil exchange between you and Ant." Gray kissed his teeth.

They made sure Rain sat right next to me. She looked so sad and confused, almost like she wanted to help me. Just pathetic.

"I say we cut through the chase and snatch her eyes out then feed 'em to her. That's what we did to muthafuckas like her back in the day."

Gramps' old ass was upset. Big Mama nodded her head in agreement. You could see the hurt in her eyes as well. Being the asshole I was, I smiled and waved at them. I knew it was over for me, so I wasn't going to just lie down for these niggas.

"What did you do, Harmony?"

"Rain, stop actin' so delusional and dumb. I was the one who destroyed yo place and sent you the package." I shook my head. "Learn to read the room."

Gray must have searched my car because I noticed the left-over black roses that were in the truck of it were now in a beautiful vase, serving as the centerpiece on the table.

"She's not delusional or dumb. My daughter is one of the sweetest, kindest people you could ever meet, and you didn't deserve her love or friendship.You're pure evil, and I hope you burn in hell." Momma Deb had her panties all in a bunch.

"Why? Just tell me why, Harmony." Rain had tears streaming down her plump cheeks.

"Gray shoulda been wit' me not you. That's why!" I slammed my hand down on the table and leaned forward. "You already had everythin'. All I wanted was him but nooooo. He desired you, perfect Rain. The girl who does no wrong and makes friends wit' everyone. The apple of her daddy's eye, and her mom's sweet girl. No one ever called me sweet girl." I let out a wicked laugh. "Did you let him know you're not so perfect after all? That someone else dwells in yo head?"

Wham!

Rain punched me so hard in the face, I flew back in my seat and onto the floor. She jumped on top of me and proceeded to beat the brakes off my ass. I didn't even get a chance to bite the bitch. She just delivered blow after blow, making me see stars.

Chapter Thirteen

RAIN

I kept beating on Harmony until Gray finally pulled me off of her. The amount of rage flowing through my body was indescribable. This was the person who I shared the majority of my life with. The one I called my sister and loved. My parents welcomed her into our home and treated her as their own. She knew everything about me and all my secrets. To find out she could betray me in such a way was unimaginable.

"You're a disgrace to sisterhood. All this over a man, who you neva had the chance of bein' wit'."

Harmony slowly got up off the floor. She wiped the blood from her mouth.

"That musta been Storm 'cause Rain could neva," she joked.

My mom jumped up to go after Harmony, but my dad stopped her.

"Gray already knows, so if you thought you had some tea to spill here, bitch, you don't, only yo blood." Harmony eyes widened.

"You just gone sit there and let 'em do this to me? Really?" We all looked around to see who Harmony was talking to. "Bear, do somethin'!"

When she said his name, my mouth dropped open.

"What the fuck goin' on, bruh?" Ant asked. "Is this the bitch you was keepin' on the low?"

We all knew Bear was messing around with someone, but he would never say who it was or bring her around. His ass said she was for the streets, and it wasn't anything serious.

"Nigga, is you fuckin' wit her or not? You need to say somethin' and say it quick." Gray raised up from his seat.

"Yes he is. We've been fuckin' around for the last year. Tell 'em, Bear." Harmony's face was all lumped up.

"I had no idea she was obsessed wit' you, Gray." Bear hung his head.

"Bruh, fuck that part. What's the reason for keepin' it a secret? That shit don't sit right wit' me. You look suspect as hell right now."

"Me either," Ant added. "Even after we found out she was the one doin' shit to Rain, you still kept quiet. Yo ass shoulda said somethin' then. Did you know she was bat shit crazy?"

"It's not even like that. Harmony and I hooked up one night after we all hung out on some drunk shit. We both had a good time and kept seein' each other. She suggested we keep it hush. I agreed 'cause I knew how Ant felt 'bout her," Bear explained.

Everyone was still in shock and disbelief when the doorbell rang.

"I can't take any more surprises." I rubbed my temples.

Gray went to get the door while I waited in suspense. He came back in with my therapist.

"What is she doin' here?" I questioned. "There's nothin' wrong wit' me." I looked over at my mom.

"Sweet girl, she's not here for you. Ms. Robinson is here for Harmony. Gray will explain everything to you later."

Ms. Robinson had a bunch of paperwork in her hand.

"The fuck she is." Harmony reached for her phone.

I snatched it before she could and slammed it on the table, over and over again until the screen cracked. She scowled up her face, and I punched her in it again.

"Come on. Take a walk with me." My mom wrapped her hand around my waist.

When we got into the hallway, I broke down crying. My heart was shattered into a thousand pieces. She held me in her arms and rubbed my back.

"But why, mom? I didn't do anythin' to deserve this. All I did was love her. I thought she loved me back. It was like she was tryin' to drive me crazy."

"I think that was her goal. I'm glad Gray was able to get information out of Jamal. He pointed them in her direction," my mom explained.

"So, he was in on it too?" I felt like I would pass out.

"Gray will explain it all to you later. Right now, my only concern is you."

"Is she okay?" My dad came into the hallway.

"Yes, she's just upset. It's a lot to take in at one time."

"I see she used that right hook I taught her." He laughed.

"Y'all havin' a family meetin' without me?" Gray joined us.

"You know what needs to be done with Bear, right? He knows more than he's sayin'." My dad spoke sternly.

"I'mma handle it." There was a sadness in Gray's eyes I had never seen before.

"If his brother has a problem with it, let me know." They walked away, leaving Gray and I alone.

"The people we loved the most betrayed us." The tears flowed freely.

Gray wiped them away and kissed my lips.

"Yeah, the shit is fucked up, but such is life. Everyone ain't meant to come along as you rise to the top."

"So, what happens now?" I questioned.

"Nothin' you need to worry 'bout. Let me see yo hand." Gray kissed my swollen knuckles. "It's a good thing yo ass a nurse."

"I can move my fingers and make a fist, so nothin' is broken. I'll put some ice on it. See what happens when you are fine like wine?"

"No, what?"

"Two women become mutually obsessed wit' you and have to fight." I smiled.

"Well, I'm glad the best woman won."

Even though Gray and I getting together turned our lives upside down, I would do it all over again. My best friend was now my lover and protector. A love like this only comes around once in a lifetime. I'm glad I didn't let it pass me by.

Epilogue

GRAY

THREE YEARS LATER...

"Kace, hold mommy's hand."

Rain had already exited the car and was standing on the sidewalk. She reached down to grab our two-year-old son's hand after I removed him from the car seat and put him down.

"Otay, daddy," he responded.

We were at Gramps and Big Mama's house for Sunday dinner. They were already standing in the doorway. It was always a fight between the two to see who Kace would go to. Big Mama won every time. Today was no different.

"He only goes to you 'cause he thinks yo big ass titties are bouncy balls." Gramps was always talking shit.

"Mmmmm, it smells like peach cobbler in here." Ant started dancing once we made it inside.

He had been at the house all day helping me get the nursery together, so he decided to come have dinner with us. Kira kept calling him the entire time, making sure he was still with me, but we got it done. Rain and I were expecting our second child in two more months. It was a girl this time. We still hadn't decided on her name.

"Yeah, and I made you yo own this time. This way the rest of us can have some too," Big Mama informed him.

It was rough for a minute after I had to lay his brother down, but Ant understood how the game was played. It took him two years to come back around. He missed our wedding and my son being born. Bear wasn't just his brother, but his twin. They shared a bond that was unique, and I understood Ant needed space and time, so I gave him that. The shit was emotional for me as well. I don't believe for one second Bear knew Harmony was obsessed with me, but he admitted knowing she was the one who left the package. He tracked her phone and saw she was at the Ellington's house at three in the morning on the day the package showed up.

This nigga didn't want to tell on her because she had his ass pussy whipped. Once Jamal revealed the reason why Harmony could be the one we were looking for, Bear felt played. He wanted her caught at that point, but didn't think she would tell us about them.

Loyalty was everything in our world, and Bear heard me tell people that all the time. Harmony could have mentally or physically harmed Rain, and this nigga knew it was her and said nothing over some ass. It made me question everything about him. Even though what he did was fucked up, I wasn't going to kill someone who I considered family over no bitch. We just would have had to part ways.

Mr. Ellington rushed to the decision of ending Bear because he was emotionally involved. He was a businessman like me and operated above the law as well, so loyalty was everything to him too. But if Rain wasn't involved, Mr. Ellington would have done an intense investigation into Bear, and that was exactly what I did.

Come to find out, for the last year he had been skimming from the top and cheating the cleanup crew out of their payments. Bear always wanted to stay behind at locations because after we left he would go back inside and get the money he failed to tell us was there or leave the cleanup crew less than what they were supposed to be paid.

Once I confronted Bear, he admitted to doing it. We split everything in thirds, so I couldn't understand why he would steal from us. When this muthafucka told me he did it to support Harmony, I was at a loss for words. The new car she suddenly had came from Bear. She stopped working once they started fucking, but still acted like she had a job to save face. This nigga covered her rent and bills and anything else she asked for. She was living the life she wanted, but it still wasn't enough because it wasn't with me.

When the day came for me to finally handle Bear, I was so fucked up I couldn't even pull the trigger. Bear was given the opportunity to choose his demise, and he chose a lethal injection, so it would be fast and painless. We chopped it up before I administered it to him. Both of us shed some tears talking about all the good times we shared. Bear even cracked a joke about me having to drive myself everywhere now. He understood the errors of his ways, but it didn't make the situation easier for either one of us.

Watching someone I loved take his last breath was the worst pain I ever experienced. After it was over, I had Bear's body taken to a funeral home. His family was able to give him a proper send off that I paid for. Ant told his family he died of a heart attack. His mom didn't deserve to have her heart burden with the truth.

After finding out the whole truth, killing Harmony would have been too easy. We forced her to sign the paperwork Ms. Robinson drew up, which committed her to a psychiatric facility permanently. Ms. Robinson was on their board of directors and made sure Harmony had a bed that night. Since she thought it was funny to play with someone's mental health, she could live with the same people she ridiculed for the rest of her life.

Knock! Knock!

I went to get the door while Rain got her and Kace situated.

"We saw y'all pull up. Where's my babies?" Miss Deb asked.

"In the livin' room." She rushed past me.

"Hey, son," Mr. Ellington greeted me.

"Wassup, boss man."

Our relationship became even stronger after I married Rain.

I was now responsible for his most prized possession. We also spent a lot of time together since Kace was born. He had everyone wrapped around his little finger.

It felt good to be surrounded by family. We all gathered in the dining room to enjoy the delicious meal Big Mama prepared for everyone.

"She'll come." Rain reached over and rubbed my hand.

I was staring at the empty place setting and wondered if my mom would keep her promise. She was able to get it together enough to come to our wedding but disappeared after that. Still to this day, my mom never laid eyes on my son.

Last night my mom called me and said she was finally ready to get the help she needed. I told her if she showed up for Sunday dinner, I would take care of everything else. I wanted her to be able to see her grandchildren grow up. It was my mom's second chance at being a parent. She missed out on me, but could assist with Kace and his sister.

As everyone made their plates, there was another knock at the door. This time Gramps went and answered it. When he walked back in with my mom behind him, a lump formed in my throat. My family was finally complete and life was good. I couldn't ask for anything more.

The End!

Author Charisse C. Carr Catalog:

A Romantic Entanglement: Autumn and Knowledge Story
https://amzn.to/3PjfagG

A Romantic Entanglement: Autumn and Knowledge Story 2
https://amzn.to/3AUOsaD

A Countdown To His Love
https://amzn.to/3CbVXJL

Harper & Stone: A Family Affair
https://bit.ly/442pD8f

Mali & Chaquille: A Dangerous Hood Love
https://amzn.to/3hQUf9i

Mali & Chaquille: A Dangerous Hood Love 2
https://amzn.to/3DlGBTD

Series

Kane & Candy: A Romantic Entanglement
https://amzn.to/3yUKnSk

A Romantic Entanglement: Autumn and Knowledge Story
https://amzn.to/3PjfagG

A Romantic Entanglement: Autumn and Knowledge Story 2
https://amzn.to/3AUOsaD

A Countdown To His Love
https://amzn.to/3CbVXJL

Harper & Stone: A Family Affair
https://bit.ly/442pD8f

Mali & Chaquille: A Dangerous Hood Love

https://amzn.to/3hQUf9i
Mali & Chaquille: A Dangerous Hood Love 2
https://amzn.to/3DlGBTD
Toxic Traits: A Collection of Domestic Violence Short Stories
https://a.co/d/f9CgFQh
The Asaad Brothers
https://a.co/d/7UxFfq8
The Asaad Brother: A Hitta's Revenge
https://a.co/d/2ufRR7O
Breathless
https://a.co/d/40FbH4i
Breathless 2
https://a.co/d/dayCOoR

Social Media:

C lick on the link below to follow me on Facebook!
https://www.facebook.com/profile.php?id=
100077944875169&mibextid=eHce3h
Click on the link below to follow me on Instagram!
https://www.instagram.com/authorcharisseccarr?igsh=
Z3FtcWtwdjl6ZWt6&utm_source=qr
Click on the link below to follow me on TikTok!
https://www.tiktok.com/@authorcharisseccarr?_t=8ibAdd
JaArz&_r=1

Coming Soon!!!

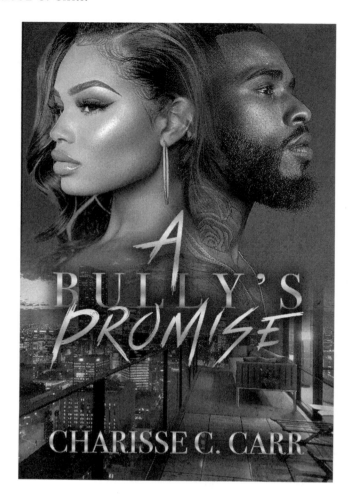

Made in the USA
Columbia, SC
06 December 2024

48624158R00076